A Robin's Pageant

ELIZABETH DOUGHERTY

A Robin's Pageant   Copyright © 2018 by Elizabeth Dougherty

ISBN: 9781980516316

Printed in the United States of America

for my grandmothers
and for every mother who has lost a child

Every morning, March through November, the backyard landscape is flocked with robins. There is pageantry in their masses, but they are truly common birds. We are, most of us, as ordinary as the robin, living our lives against the backdrop of the world's drama. Yet what soul does not marvel, does not pull up sharp, at the discovery of a robin's egg in spring – that startling, unrivaled blue against its backdrop of brown and drab. This stunning gift, produced by a bird so plain, is clearly proof of the extraordinary undercurrents of ordinary life. Each of us, robins all, have something beautiful and startling to offer to the pageant of the world.

Louella

One

Loss is inevitable, an inescapable truth. The grief that follows and the need to bear it, those are two more truths. But how? That question is answered differently by each one of us. How will you furrow despite your sorrows? Will you be able to plant life and grief together side by side? Because that's what can tear you in two, the plowing of this pathway through your soul. Will the sky above you expand to let in light again, or will it press itself in, heavy all around you, allowing nothing new to grow?

Grief and joy, the weights of time, propel our lives forward and back, and forward again. The moments of my life are all but used up now. All these moments, all the days, have stacked and compressed like layers of so much sediment, until each has become the merest sliver. Most of them are regular, necessary rock, but some are shiny and precious. Those are the few that will remain, while the rest just silt away.

Sam was my second husband. We grew up in the same town, and in my younger days I would have laughed out loud if I'd been told I'd marry him someday. Sam Purcell? But once we were reacquainted, he told me he had loved me from the first time he'd seen me, when he was eight and I was already fourteen. This should have been hard to believe, but Sam was always a man of few words, and none of them wasted. Where I could be over-talkative, not trusting the vacuum of unfilled silences between people, Sam was quiet and deliberate, and I learned to pay close attention when he pronounced something.

We met each other again in the autumn of 1943. I was working as the counter girl at Good's Grocery and General Merchandise, owned and operated by Mr. Wallace Good. I'd been just a girl when I started working there, barely past twenty years old. At forty, I was hardly a girl anymore, but since the round of customers was the same most days in our small Pennsylvania town, we all continued to see each other as we had been, not as we were. In my solitary state, I was still the same *girl*, the same Louella Reams I had always been.

I worked at the store each day from morning until closing. For so many years, my days had been seamlessly interchangeable, but something shifted that autumn of 1943.

Every evening I walked home along the three-mile stretch of quiet road between the edge of town and my family's farm. As I savored the solitude of my walks home that fall, deep in thought, Sam would drive past me on his own way home. He lived with his mother at the end of the same road in the largest house in Osceola Mills. It was beautiful in its own imposing way, but I wouldn't have wanted to live there myself. Built of ochre-colored bricks, it was all sharp edges and hard corners. I couldn't picture much sunshine penetrating any of the shadowed, lofty rooms I imagined inside. The few times when I did visit that house, once I knew Sam better, I learned that my imagination had been accurate. Warmth and light did not much live there.

I'd always known who Sam was. Everyone knew who everyone was in Osceola Mills, and the Purcell family was the most prominent family in our county. But I didn't really know him. For one thing, he was younger than I was. Also, he'd gone away to college, which was not something many people from our town did, not having money or inclination. But the Purcells had money, and Sam had the inclination. He was very intelligent, and not really cut out for farm work or physical labor. When Sam's father had died, since there were no other children, Sam had come back to live with his mother. People who did leave, who found a new place in the world, usually didn't turn up again to stay, so Sam's coming back was also unusual. Even once he was back, he worked at some sort of technical job in another town. He was just *other* in all the ways you could be *other* then, in the place we were from.

Each evening on that shared stretch of road, Sam would slow his dark blue Cadillac to a crawl as he approached.

"Would you like a ride?" he'd call through the open window. He would say it just loud enough for me to hear him above the hum and purr of the motor.

Each time he stopped, I did the same inward groan. He's just asking to be polite, I would tell myself. Even though I didn't know him well, I knew enough to know he'd always been quiet and awkward. The idea of trying to carry on a conversation with Sam Purcell for even a mile or two down the road didn't appeal to me at all, especially compared to the singular conversation already going on in my head.

But one damp evening, the sky was especially dark, and a chilly wind bit at the backs of my legs. This time when Sam slowed down next to me and asked if I wanted a ride, I said yes, thank you. Those three words turned out to be some of the most important words I would ever say.

Even though his offer was the same as all the other times before, my answer was not. As soon as I'd said yes, Sam looked stricken, filling me immediately with regret. If only I could unsay it, because he wasn't too sure what to do with my acceptance. His eyebrows shot up into his sparse hairline until they'd almost left his face, and his mouth hung open for a second. Then he recovered himself, closed his mouth, and turned the engine off right there in the middle of the empty road. He unfolded himself from his seat and came around to the passenger side to open the door for me.

Sam was tall, very tall. He was ungainly. He moved cautiously, like a giraffe at dusk, a large and gentle animal in the presence of the unknown or unseen. I had seen a wildlife picture like this once, giraffes on the savanna, in a school book. Watching Sam get out of the car that evening gave me the same feeling I'd had when I looked at that picture, like I needed to be very still and quiet. I would learn as I knew him better that Sam always moved like that to some degree, whether nervous or not. He was never all that comfortable in his own body even in most easy circumstances.

Once I was seated, Sam closed the door for me and moved slowly back around to the driver's side. He got into his own seat, pulled the door closed, and restarted the engine. I felt struck dumb. I talked all day long to people at the store about things of not much consequence, filling time and space, but now I couldn't collect my thoughts enough to string two sensible words together. Why did this awkward, quiet young man make me so self-conscious?

"Ah, it's just down on the right, the white house," was what I finally managed to say.

"I know it. Pass it every day." He said it simply without a hint of sarcasm, and he didn't look at me as he spoke.

I tried again, feeling like I had to say something else.

"I was so sorry to hear about your father. Pneumonia? My mother told me." Though his father had died six years earlier, this was really all I could think of to say.

"Thank you," Sam replied, without seeming to think my comment was out of place. This time he did glance over at me. His face had not changed expression, but his eyes held sadness. He must miss his father, I thought. His mother had the reputation of being a difficult woman.

"I'm sorry about your father, also. And I'm sorry about what happened to Holland," Sam said in return.

My own father had died two years earlier. My other, deeper loss stretched much farther back, twenty-one years, almost half my lifetime ago. My young husband, Holland, had died two months after we were married and eight months before our son would be born. Even after so many years, the emptiness of it was always with me, so Sam's condolence didn't seem out of place, either.

Sam said nothing about the baby, but this didn't surprise me. It was possible he didn't know, though more likely that he did. Even if he knew, the loss of my child was not easily talked about, even out of courtesy. Nobody, not even my own family, said anything to me about the baby. Ever. In those twenty-one years, my heart had shaped itself into a stone of compressed sadness, loneliness, and regret. The stone was mossed over, padded with the passing of those years, but hard and heavy still.

"Thank you," I said. I swallowed hard.

And then we had reached the farm. I guess I really shouldn't have been so worried about filling two miles of road with conversation. Sam pulled all the way into the rutted drive between the barn and the house, and then he turned off the engine again. I was sure I saw the kitchen curtain flutter as my mother peered out the window to see why there was a car in our yard. I hoped Sam hadn't noticed. He seemed fully occupied in searching for where to place his large, boat-like feet in the hardened mud of the lane as he came around to open my door.

I planted my foot solidly on the ground, determined not to lose my balance as I stepped out of the car. I think most men would have reached a hand out to help me, but Sam just stood there, one hand still on the door handle, the other hanging at his side. That was fine with me. I hadn't had the touch of a man's hand to help me in that way in a long time. Once I was standing next to him, I took in again how very tall he was. I was a tall woman, but the top of my head barely came even with his shoulder as we shared that awkward moment. Again, I didn't know what to say.

"Well, ah, thank you so much for the ride home."

Did this situation require any other kind of acknowledgment? I surely wasn't going to invite him in.

"And say hello to your mother," I finished limply. My comment lacked sincerity, but I was sure his mother, from what I knew of her, wouldn't care one way or the other about my greeting.

"Yes, thank you," said Sam. "I mean, you're welcome, and thank you for allowing me to give you a ride."

"Well, good night then."

I nodded and started to pick my way across the lane to the house.

"Good night, Louella."

Louella. This startled me, Sam saying my name, and I stopped. It was my name, of course. I heard it day in and day out, but it surprised me when I heard Sam say it, almost as if I hadn't been sure he knew it. I looked back at him and gave him a small smile, then turned back again toward the house. I couldn't watch as he folded himself back into the car, but I heard the engine start just as I reached the door, then the sound of the tires rumbling back out of the lane.

The kitchen smelled richly of roasting chicken, a warm welcome on that blustery night. Before I'd even closed the door all the way, my mother was in front of me, hands on hips, mouth in a satisfied line.

"Who was that out there? Was that Sam Purcell?" she demanded.

I knew she'd been looking out the window.

"Yes," I answered. "Yes, it was. He gave me a ride home."

"What made you finally let him?" my mother asked.

I had only mentioned Sam once to my mother, the first time he'd offered me a ride, but somehow, she knew he'd asked me every night since. My mother had extra perception about many things, which I guess is a skill that accumulates from raising a lot of children. More than once she'd said, "Why don't you just let him give you a ride home? He's a nice young man. You could do a lot worse, you know."

I knew my mother meant well, but I didn't think she could fully understand the sustenance I gathered on my walks home, sorting through my stockpiled collection of thoughts. Like marbles, I held them up to the light one by one for truer examination, to find the worlds within.

My mother was different. Doing, not thinking, was her usual life method. She was a brisk woman, the definition of a farm woman. She'd been raised on a farm, then she'd gotten married at sixteen and moved to another farm. Then she'd became the mother of nine farm children. It seemed like my mother had been a life-long grownup. Even with nine children, she didn't really ever talk about her childhood or recognize in any of us the child she had been. She'd probably never had two moments of quiet contemplation to rub together in her whole life.

No, I don't think my mother held marbles up to the light very often, so when she asked me about accepting a ride home from Sam, I didn't elaborate or analyze. I answered simply.

"I was cold," I said.

It was true. I had little warmth in my life during those long years after my too short marriage, after my young husband died so swiftly. I went through the motions of my days because I had to, but I was always lonely. Even surrounded by my family and the people I'd known all my life, I felt alone.

Mr. Good had given me the job at his store after Holland died and the baby was gone, once I had resurfaced. Wallace Good was a caring man. Soft inside and out and all the way through, this was how my mother always described him. His caring ways were evident in his leniency toward his customers, who were also his friends and neighbors. Even when they couldn't afford to pay in full for what their children and families really needed, Good's customers never went without. They never took advantage of Wallace Good's generosity, either. I think this was because we all had to live in the same small town, and life had taught us it would all come around.

Whether Mr. Good gave me the store job to fill my own need or his, I was never too sure. It was probably some of both. The store was the only large one in town. It was always busy, and he always needed extra hands, even with his wife and two daughters working there. His daughters, Irene and Idelle, were around my age, and Wallace Good could probably see shadows of my plight in the futures of his own girls. Fate is not particular, at least not in a way we can often see, and widows are easily made. He felt for me as a father would, and he gave me a job. It was a destination for each day, a time and place where I would have no other choice but to move and talk and participate.

It did help, a bit. I could see life going on all around me, warm-blooded, colorful, and loud, but I saw it like it was taking place behind a piece of cheesecloth or a screen. I witnessed all the scenes but without any intensity. I could almost reach out and make contact. Almost. But there was always that layer in between. How could I ever have known it would be a man like Sam who would lead me down the path of re-connection?

Two

Osceola Mills had its share of beautiful days. Balmy
spring afternoons scented with lilacs. White winter
mornings, crystallized and silent. On those days the town
was magically self-contained, suspended like a perfect
water droplet. But those days were few and far between,
and on most days the town was drab, suspended less
beautifully. It was held firmly in place by its removed
location, the cycles of its industry, and a kind of
momentum-less rotation of children becoming the same
adults their parents had been. Maybe it was really that
way, or maybe it just felt that way to me, caught as I was
in my own web of repetition. This was where I grew up,
where I still was in 1943, and where I met Sam again.

Our family of eleven was a medium-sized family in
that time and place. There were two boys, three girls,
then two more boys, then another girl, and finally one
more boy. We never had much quiet in our house. By the
time I met Sam, my brother Carrol and I were the only
ones still living on the farm with my mother. Work, war,
marriage, and illness – the whim and variety of life – had
taken all the others, and then my father, too.

My brothers George and Marshall both fought in the
Great War, and both died at the Somme. I think the fact
of their being together in a death so far from home gave
my mother some small comfort. George had sent her a

silky handkerchief from France, banded red, white, and blue like a small French flag, which she kept on the table by her bed forever after, a sentimental reminder for the generally unsentimental woman my mother was. A younger me had been envious of my oldest brothers' opportunity to launch into the wider world, maybe even a little envious of their heroic deaths. But the haunt never left the eyes of the men who did return from that horrible war, and the older me knew my brothers would have come home equally wretched, wrenched from any sense of complacency or completeness. We would have understood each other well then, George and Marshall and the older me, but they were not coming back to the farm, no matter how much I wished it.

After George and Marshall came Angelica, then me, and then Lenore. Lenore married a man named Alfred. They lived on a farm in Madera and had five children, all girls. We usually visited them at Christmastime, and they came back over to visit us once or twice a summer. Angelica had married a man named Arthur. He was a professor, and they lived in State College. They were with us at Christmastime at Lenore's, but we did not visit them in State College. I never once went there.

After Lenore was Austin and then John. Even though they were two years apart, you could just about think they were the same person, they looked so much alike. They both worked in the Plane Mine in Woodland, about twelve miles from us, and their wives, Ruth and Ellen, were actual twin sisters. Austin and John each had two boys and a girl, in that order. They lived next door to each other, and their families were very tight.

After John, there was little Edith, who died of diphtheria right after her second birthday. In my mind's eye, there lived a vision of Edith's round toddler face looking up at me solemnly, big brown eyes steady. That was all that was left of Edith.

And finally, there was Carrol, still on the farm with us in 1943 despite the war. Carrol had escaped the draft by the sheer good fortune of having chronic stomach ulcers. At least my mother and I saw it as good fortune. Carrol viewed his 4-F as very bad luck. He was still young enough to want military adventure, to claim the bravery, even considering the war time deaths of our two older brothers. Carrol never knew George and Marshall, and their heroic absence fed his restlessness.

At nineteen, Carrol had become the man of the family when our father died after being kicked in the chest by our mule. Why we kept that mule for so long, I don't really know. He was nasty, the only thing he did was eat. Carrol shot the mule without a second thought after he kicked my father, but my father died anyway the next day. Carrol was ashamed by his reactive, out-of-character violence. I felt worse for him than for the loss of my father, who was a gruff man. He was the type of man who used gestures more than words to say what he needed us to do or what he thought of us. To him we were all just mouths to feed. I think he'd had a different, better way with my older brothers than with the rest of us, but it was gone once they were. My mother didn't seem to mourn my father much either. She was worn down by so many losses already. With his death, the rhythm of our lives changed little. If anything, it was less pinched, and I was mostly relieved.

The town had not changed much between the time I was a little girl and a grown-up woman. It was a compact collection of small businesses and buildings. Smallish houses filled the surrounding streets, with farmhouses and cultivated farmland dividing the hills for miles beyond. It was very similar to most small, rural American towns in the early twentieth century, at least any of the ones I had visited.

Good's store sat at the intersection of the two main roads, Curtain Street and Stone Street, to the north and south. Further along was a barber shop, the post office, and the fire station. The Methodist church anchored one end of Curtain Street, imposing in its brightness. Its sharp, white steeple jabbed at the sky, and its solid brick manse lurked behind it.

Everyone in town went to the Methodist church. The children in our family had always taken up the entire fourth pew on the left. My mother and father sat in the pew behind us ready to poke a cold finger between the shoulder blades of any child not upright and alert throughout the entire long service. My parents often reminded us how they had been made to sit through two or three services' worth of preaching at a time. When they were growing up, a visiting pastor came to church one Sunday a month, and on those Sundays, you were churched enough to last the four weeks until the next visit.

The smaller Catholic Church sat directly across the street from the Methodist church. It was a brooding presence with intensely-colored windows and a dark, shadowed doorway. It had been built by and for the Irish and Italian railroad workers about fifty years before I was born, but during my time it stood empty and quiet. A priest and a few workers would arrive to take care of the building twice a year. Otherwise, it kept its own company. As a child I'd always wondered if the doors were locked in between those priestly visits, but I was never brave enough to try them and find out.

The schoolhouse stood at the other end of Curtain Street, another solid brick building, single-storied and serious. It held the first through eighth grades in two large rooms, with a small library room in between. The school was easily my favorite place as a child. We had only about sixty students and two teachers, young Miss Reynolds and the widowed Mrs. Smythe. For many kids, the Osceola school was as much education as they ever got. After eighth grade, a lot of them filtered out of school altogether. The boys worked on their family farms or at the brickyard, which employed most of the men in town. The girls helped their mothers with the housework until they got married themselves. Only a handful of students moved on to the high school over in Madera.

From the start, I was determined to continue to the high school. So far, in our family only my sister, Angelica, had gone on. My teachers recognized something I hadn't known was in me until I started school, a spark just needing to be coaxed along. We didn't have many books at the farm, but I learned to read quickly at school. I discovered how much I loved books, loved the idea of new ideas. I stretched the boundaries of my small world and learned for the sake of learning. In school, in books, I'd found a place where I could be more than just one of the Reams kids, a place where I could be more than someone's sister, someone's daughter. There I could be just Louella.

I moved through all the grades rapidly. I finished eighth grade when I was twelve, and I went on to the high school like I'd hoped. I even daydreamed of becoming a teacher. Then I was reined back home, the shape of my future assumed for a long time. After that, the pull I felt toward school and the learning world was like the memory of a vivid dream, known in every detail, but without the substance of reality. Not a place you could ever go back to, not one that had ever really existed at all.

Other than the school and the Methodist church, the largest presence in our lives and the life of the town was the brickyard. The Osceola Mills Silica Brickworks churned out sturdy, fine-grained, ochre-colored bricks used all over Pennsylvania, and even through Ohio and Maryland. The brickworks buildings and yard were on Stone Street, all the way at the north end of town. I passed them every evening on my walk home from the store. Loyal Purcell, Sam's grandfather, had founded the company, and he'd made quite a lot of money by town standards.

My father had worked at the brickyard once my older brothers were gone and there weren't enough hands to work our farm, and Carrol worked there, too. Looking at it this way, my family and Sam's had already been connected for quite a long time. Yet the gulf between the Purcell and Reams families couldn't have been much wider.

Three

We had six milk cows, a flock of chickens, a large garden,
plus a house to take care of, and there always seemed to
be a lot left to do when I got back from the store each
night. My walk home was the only time I really had to
myself to think my thoughts all the way through, to sort
through the collection I kept in the little pocket at the
back of my mind.

The day after Sam gave me that first ride home, I
didn't have time to give him another thought. It was
sunny and clear. After the chilly, wet day before, the
change in weather drew lots of customers into the store to
socialize as much as to buy things. I spent the day talking,
talking, talking. As I walked home, I slowed my pace to
sort through my thoughts, bathing in the milder air,
breathing it in, storing it up for later.

Carrol had come into the store that busy day along
with everyone else. He came over from the brickyard
about half the time to spend his lunch break with me.
We'd eat sitting on tall stools behind the back counter.
Shelving stretched up the wall to the ceiling behind us,
filled with bolts of fabric, tubes of knitting needles, skeins
of yarn, boxes of buttons, rolls of plain and fancy ribbon.
Sometimes my mother came in, too. Then we'd all eat

lunch at a little table in the back room while I kept an ear out for any lunchtime customers.

"Louella, a telephone," Carrol had exclaimed when he arrived that day, as if it were a thought all on its own.

"What?" I'd replied automatically, listening with only one ear. I was rewinding ribbons onto their spools from where they were snaked across the counter. It was typical of Carrol to burst out with ideas and exclamations at times when I was already in the middle of something else.

"A telephone," Carrol said again as he strode purposefully over to me. "I really think it's time we got a telephone, is what I meant. Then we could talk to anyone, at any time, and there would never be an emergency."

He came around the end of the counter and sat himself on the stool next to me as I continued to untangle ribbons. It wasn't the first time Carrol had tried to talk to me about getting a telephone. A lot of the businesses in town and a few of our neighbors had them then, but we didn't, and my mother wasn't at all interested in getting one. Mr. Good had a phone at the store. He always seemed to be shouting into it or asking callers to repeat themselves. I would rather just talk to people face to face. You couldn't see a questioning smile or a quizzically raised eyebrow through a phone line. Besides, why did Carrol think that just because you could hear someone's voice on the other end of the line, that would mean emergencies would cease to occur. A voice coming out of thin air had no power over the concrete world. But even as I shrugged Carrol's enthusiasm away, I felt unsettled by the gleam in his eye.

I walked home that night deep in thought about change in the form of telephones and so many other things. Change, called progress, was coming whether we installed a phone or not. I weighed and balanced more than just the changes themselves. I considered Carrol's enthusiasm for the modern forces shaping his adult life, which was only just beginning. His readiness to plunge fully into everything made me uneasy. It made me feel old. The routines of my daily life were unchanged after so many years. I did not love them, I did not loathe them, but their steady repetition was at least reliable.

When I was Carrol's age, on the edge of my own adulthood, a piece of me had wanted to detach, too. I had wanted to untangle from the routines holding everyone and everything firmly in place in our small part of the world, but expectation and fear had stopped me. Later that sameness and solidity were what held me together and upright. No, I didn't share my brother's shiny-eyed fervor for telephones or anything else that might cause my world to shift. Instead, I felt myself brushing up against the edge of fear, like bracing for the moment when you turn your head and grit your teeth to tear off a bandage. I felt fingers poised, ready to rip.

Of course, I know better now. Everything within and around us is always changing. It's only when we look back through the kaleidoscope, the shifting shapes and colors of the years, that we realize the extent of all the change surrounding us, seeping through our lives even while we feel like we're merely treading water.

I was so deeply lost in my own head that night thinking about change, I didn't hear Sam's car until it was right up alongside me, and he was asking, not quite as quietly as the night before, if I wanted a ride. This time, Sam said *Louella* first. I nearly jumped out of my skin. That expression has new meaning once you really experience it.

I recovered quickly enough to reach for the door handle before Sam could get out and try to do it for me. Something inside me decided in that split second that it would be fine to ride home with him again, but his getting out and opening the door would make it seem like more of an ordeal, which I didn't want it to be. It would be much better if I opened the door myself. If I could read anything on Sam's still unfamiliar face, I think he was relieved that I was quicker than he was.

"Was it a busy day at the store then?" Sam asked without looking at me, once I was in and we were on our way.

"It was," I replied, turning my head just slightly in his direction.

I liked the way his sandy hair flopped over his high forehead a bit, softening his serious profile. I caught the edge of a smile pulling his mouth at my precise, two-word answer. As I shifted my coat around me, my uneasiness receded. All my worries about change and the future lifted. Up, up, and away from me they went, and I couldn't quite put my finger on what had been unsettling me so intensely just moments before.

I hadn't ridden beside a man who wasn't related to me in a long time. Sam was such a contrast to Holland. As a boy and a young man, Holland had always commanded attention. He'd always had something to say. He thought out loud and talked expressively. He was so *alive*, until he wasn't. Since he'd died, I'd veered toward quiet, toward stillness. Although I didn't realize it yet, I would find that same kind of stillness in Sam.

The third night, when I heard Sam's car coming down the road, I turned around to wait as he slowed down and then stopped alongside me. I got in even before he said anything. It was that easy. I almost couldn't believe that just a few days before I'd been practically speechless riding home with him. My mother had been right, as mothers sometimes are. Sam was a very nice young man. I could do much worse.

Sam and I continued this routine every evening for several weeks. On each ride we found new subjects to fill what had been such uncertain space that first night. Our conversation was measured and steady, never rushed. Our companionship was not a flirtation, not then.

Sam asked me if I liked my job at the store, and I told him I enjoyed working in the middle of all that activity, even though I didn't like to be the center of anything myself. I'd worked there for so long I couldn't imagine what my days would be like without the store as part of them.

I asked Sam a lot about his job. He worked for a man who owned a radio sales and repair shop in Madera. Sam told me about studying electrical engineering for the short time he was in State College. He loved tinkering with radio parts, and his father had gotten him a radio when they were a brand-new thing to buy. Sam said his dad had probably suspected he would immediately take the radio apart to figure out how it worked. Sam did just that, and then he put it back together again, many times over. He told me how satisfying it was to discover later that his messing about with all the working parts of something was really engineering, and that it could be useful in a real job.

After jobs, Sam and I also talked about the brickyard, the weather, all the little details of the small-town rural life we both knew, and what we thought of it all. We realized how much we had in common at the core, growing up in that place, despite how different our lives looked on the surface. Soon I even felt comfortable enough to tease Sam a little. A few smiles, a few wry chuckles, and he seemed like a different man from the one I had gotten into the car with on that first night. As we traveled those few miles together each evening, I traveled many miles of internal road, circling closer and closer around the woman I had been years before, a woman with a warm and hopeful heart.

Four

My first husband was Holland Richards. We were married in 1922, but I knew him, as I had known of Sam, for most of my life. That's how things were in small country towns then. Maybe it's not so different now.

Holland was always a deeply kind boy. He was teaser and a jokester, but never harsh or mean-spirited. He was observant, but without judgment or an ounce of introspection. I had enough of that for us both. Even though we were different in many ways, we shared the love of new ideas, and the same type of humor. I think our place together in the world had been prepared for as long as we had known each other, just waiting for us to leave our flighty, flimsier roles as children and become solid adults. No interruption in the flow, no question of the plan. I never really considered whether my life could or would be any other way, or in any other place.

Holland and I were the same age, our birthdays only a week apart. We'd gone all through the Osceola school together. In the early grades we were friendly in the way young boys and girls can be, when we all ran through the schoolyard together as one herd. Later, we mostly ignored each other, as older boys and girls do, divided by some sort of silent but binding agreement.

Then one day, Holland walked me home without even asking. He talked to me like we were picking up the end of an earlier conversation. He started in about how much he liked the smell of barns in the autumn after the haying. He kept talking at me, and before I knew it we'd reached the spot where the road parted toward our separate farms. We were twelve then.

We walked together after that for the rest of the school year. The next year, when I went on to the high school, Holland didn't, but that didn't change our routine much. The high school kids rode to Madera in a wagon, and when we reappeared around the corner of Curtain Street each afternoon, there Holland would be, waiting. He would take my books, and we'd be on our way.

When we were fourteen, Holland's mother died of a cruel, wasting cancer. Then his father was killed in an accident at the brickyard less than a year later. His brother, Alden, who was six years older, was a medic on the front in France. The deaths of his parents and the absence of his brother sobered Holland's easy personality. He continued to live on the farm with his Aunt Marion, who had always lived with them, and we continued our walks home together, though during that time our conversations were quieter than they had been, and some days we didn't really talk at all. After some time had passed, though, and Alden returned whole and healthy, Holland's constitutional optimism took over once again. He was deepened, matured, but not made bitter.

When we were fifteen Holland started holding my hand on the way home. And at sixteen, he kissed my cheek each time we reached the place where the main road divided. When we were nineteen, we got married, and I moved from my family's farm to his. And that was that.

The November day I knew for sure I was pregnant was the same day Holland's nagging cough turned sharply unbearable. I had been counting weeks and feeling low on energy. A baby would be no surprise, and I was happy. I knew Holland would be happy, too. But when he came into the kitchen while Marion and I were washing up the breakfast dishes, I forgot to think about babies.

It was a Saturday. Holland had been outside fixing a splintered porch rail, coughing the whole time. He sat down heavily in a kitchen chair and said raggedly, "I need to see the doctor, Louella."

We had an open horse cart and a covered buggy. I drove the cart more confidently, so without asking I handed Holland an extra blanket and hitched up our horse, Roland, to the cart. Holland climbed up slowly, without comment. Marion watched silently from the front porch, brows knitted. Her anxiousness settled itself next to mine as I drove us away toward town.

Dr. Hobbs listened to Holland's breathing and told us we needed to go immediately to the new hospital in Philipsburg. He was certain it was pneumonia. He and Holland passed a look of resignation between them. It wasn't lost on me, how much they said to each other above my head without speaking.

There weren't too many cars around our parts yet in 1922, but Dr. Hobbs had one, and he drove us to the hospital himself. When we got there, we were met by two starched nurses, and Dr. Hobbs left us, believing there wasn't anything more he could do for Holland. I followed the nurses intently, trying to understand all the information and directives passing between them. Only later, in the quiet, did I realize how much I missed the reassuring presence of the familiar Dr. Hobbs. I had never been to a hospital before.

We were led to a corner room with four beds. The younger nurse made a purposeful circuit of the room, opening the three large casement windows. There were no oxygen tents at this hospital yet. Throwing all the windows wide open was thought to be the next best treatment. The flowing air, a gale of life force, was supposed to cleanse the lungs and body, to ease the breathing. We could have done that much at home, I thought flatly.

The older nurse, grey and stern, handed Holland a long hospital nightshirt and told him to change out of his own clothes. She made no move to leave the room or turn away, and her steely expression told me she wasn't used to being asked to. I lowered my eyes as Holland struggled out of his shirt and stepped unsteadily out of his trousers. I wanted to help him. I should have helped him. I was his wife. But I was frozen as I witnessed this stripping of his individuality. This is the first loss that happens when disease moves in and takes over. Holland was not Holland in that room. He was simply a patient. And I wasn't sure who or what I was.

"Are you going to remain at the hospital, Mrs. Richards?" the grey nurse asked, taking me by surprise. I was still not used to being addressed as Mrs. Richards.

"Sorry. Ah, yes, I think so."

Of course I was staying. Where else did I have to go? The nurse looked me over disapprovingly. What would have been the right answer?

"Well, if you think so, you can't stay in here. You may proceed to the waiting room. Turn left out the door. Then right at the end of the hallway, and you'll see it." She pursed her lips around her sour tone.

The younger nurse turned from where she was unloading items from a medical cabinet in the corner of the room.

"We need to do what we can to make your husband more comfortable," she said kindly. "The doctor will come down to speak with you as soon as he can."

My *husband*. I wasn't used to this word yet either. I'd had a husband for such a short, sweet time.

On wooden legs I followed the hallway until I found the waiting room. How did I feel sitting in that room waiting for Holland to die? Because I was sure that was what was going to happen. Pneumonia killed people, and it seemed to me once you were in a hospital, you were as good as dead. More than anything else in those waiting hours, I was angry. I was angry with Dr. Hobbs for bringing us there. I was angry at being there all by myself to wait and worry. I was angry at the unkind nurse. I was, most unfairly, angry at Holland for getting sick. My anger became a river, surging through me, pure and swift. The river filled my head, making my breath come as short as Holland's in the room down the hall. I wanted to throw every stick of furniture in that waiting room up against the pure white walls, but instead, all my anger stayed locked inside me. I sat very still. I tried to breathe normally and tried not to look at anyone else in that room. I didn't care who those other people were or who they were waiting for. I did not want to be counted among them.

A kind hand on my shoulder woke me. I had fallen asleep in my seat, exhausted by the violent current of my anger. My head rested back against that clean, white wall. The day had grown dim, and I found myself alone in the room except for the doctor who stood next to my chair.

"Mrs. Richards?"

He was young, older than I was but much younger than Dr. Hobbs. I sat up and shook myself more alert.

"Mrs. Richards?" he said again.

"Yes." My mouth was almost too dry to respond.

"I'm Dr. Lindquist. I wanted to let you know we've done our best to make Mr. Richards comfortable, and he's sleeping. I'm afraid now we'll just have to wait and watch. We need to let him rest as much as possible."

The sympathy in the doctor's tired eyes told me he knew my despair, my doubts. His eyes told me he was not hopeful, either. I only nodded. I knew if I spoke I wouldn't be able to stop myself from asking if Holland would die, and I knew the doctor would not tell me, even if he knew the answer.

"You may go in and sit with him, but try not to wake him," the doctor said. "Please let the nurses know if you have any questions, and they'll come find me."

I walked back down the long hallway. Was it just this morning we'd come here? I sat right up close to the bed in a ladder-backed chair. I wanted to slip my hand up underneath the blankets to find Holland's, but the doctor's reminder warned me off. Holland needed to sleep. I didn't want to risk waking him up.

All the way to the hospital with Dr. Hobbs, I had thought about how to tell Holland I was pregnant. I didn't want to tell him in the car, not like that. Then when we got to the hospital, there was no right moment, with the opening of windows, the undressing, the unsympathetic, barking nurse. Now I wasn't sure what to do. I was overwhelmed by emotion, impending grief, and exhaustion. Would it be easier or harder for Holland to leave this world knowing he was almost a father? Almost.

His rasping breaths filled the room with an unsteady rhythm, and I felt myself struggle to breathe with him. I closed my eyes and pictured a day early in September, the last wave of summer heat settling over the afternoon. We'd been married for a week. Holland ran toward me through the field behind the barn, his face pinked and sweaty. He grasped me at the waist and swung me around. What had he been laughing at? As I sat in the hard chair in that cold, sterile room, I couldn't remember what had been so funny, but I did remember the color, the warmth, the filtered sunlight, the light inside of me. On that unremarkable day, everything about our lives had been full and possible, joy within easy reach. Now, without touching him, I prayed Holland could feel me remembering that shining, laughing afternoon as he went on trying to breathe, face ashen, cheeks sunken.

The next thing I knew, I startled myself awake, almost slipping from the chair. Dusk was beginning to fill in the spaces outside. I knew I should go back to the waiting room to try to sleep. I could get myself that far. I could slip into this night, but I could not think beyond it. I would not put myself into tomorrow.

I chose the most comfortable looking chair in the waiting room, but I couldn't sleep there. I don't know how long I sat, thinking, trying not to think. Hours. Then slowly, morning sunlight layered into the room from a small, high window. Its beam seemed almost solid, and I imagined pulling myself up onto this path, following it out through the little window. I would not look back.

Dr. Lindquist came quietly into the room while I was journeying up the sunbeam. I was very glad it was not the sour nurse. The doctor's kind eyes told me all I needed to know. Before he said a word, I knew I would be going home alone.

Life is fragile and often short. I had already lost people I knew and loved, everyday people like me, like Holland. Everyone I knew had experienced death as a close companion at some turn, but now it was my turn again. This was my husband, this was Holland. None of those other lost people mattered to me that awful morning. I found no comfort in the sad company I kept. I was nineteen years old, about to be a mother, but no longer a wife. I felt like I belonged nowhere. Where would I lay down my loss? Where would I sort through my sadness?

I made my way through the funeral and burial automatically. When my brother-in-law, Alden, returned from medical school in Philadelphia for the service, he assured me I could stay on in his family's house with Aunt Marion for as long as I wanted to. Holland would have wanted me to stay, Alden said. As much as I liked Marion and knew she liked me, I could not belong in that house without Holland.

The day after the service, my mother brought me back to our farm without much discussion that I remember. I told her about the baby. I think she had already guessed I might be pregnant. She asked if Alden and Marion knew, and when I said no, she simply nodded. I took that to mean she would tell them for me.

She probably assumed that Holland had known about the baby, and I let her think it. I didn't tell her Holland had died without knowing, that I had kept it from him. If I'd had to speak those words, I think I might have died, too.

My family treated any grief by moving ahead, pushing forward with the tasks of each day, and my new grief was no different. This method seemed to work for them, seemed to work for most people I knew. Not for me. Back where I started from, I filled in the space I'd left so recently like a damaged puzzle piece. My edges did not mesh, even though they had once been cut to fit.

Five

Sam confessed his true love in late November, just before Thanksgiving. By then I'd already realized that not only could I do much worse, but there was really no man better for me. I had a lot to be thankful for.

When Sam pulled into the farm lane on that momentous evening, he turned off the engine and stared a hole in the steering wheel. I reached for the door handle to let myself out, but he cleared his throat, a sure signal to stop me.

"Louella…"

It came out a croak. By this time, I'd gotten used to the sort of somber way he said my name, but this night I sensed something different. He tried again, stronger.

"Louella, I need to say something important."

"Okay, Sam."

"Louella, I'm telling the truth when I say I have loved you since the very first time I ever saw you."

I laughed. It was awful, but I couldn't help it. It just burst out of me. Sam looked almost sick as he waited for me to say something, or to somehow take back my laugh.

"Oh Sam, I'm so sorry, I didn't mean…"

"No, don't apologize, Louella. I don't even know what I was thinking."

"Oh Sam, it's not that. It's just that you sounded so solemn about it, and the first time you saw me, I think you were eight years old! How could you have thought anything at all about me when you were eight?"

He turned toward me then, his seriousness holding steady.

"I knew it, even in an eight-year-old way," he said. "And I love you now. I mean it."

Then Sam seemed to gather strength from his own words. He appeared to grow straighter before my eyes, as if by speaking the truth he grew to believe it even more himself. He held his love out for me to choose, to accept or reject freely. And this time I didn't laugh. I believed it too.

After that night, Sam picked me up at the store every evening instead of on the road to home. We never talked about this arrangement. Like a lot of things between us, it just seemed to happen. The first time he arrived at the store, I was in the little back room out of view. I was just hanging up my shop apron and reaching for my coat when I heard the bells on the front doors jangle, even though the store was closed.

"Good evenin' there, Sam. You here for Louella then? She's in the back."

"Good evening, Mr. Good."

Lucky Sam. He got away with a handshake and a nod, I guessed by what I could hear from where I stood. No need to state his purpose. Wallace Good seemed to know it already in his all-knowing way.

Then again, maybe the whole town was talking about us, Sam and me, and I just hadn't realized it. I'd been going about my daily life at the store and then riding home with Sam each night without giving much thought to how these two pieces of my routine intersected. Other than my mother, not one single customer or neighbor, not a one, had said a word directly to me about Sam. But it was a very small town, after all.

In all those years after Holland died, and then so much loss had followed, I'd been closed in on myself in a way I could never have imagined until it happened. On the outside, I was still Louella Reams, growing older by the year just like everyone else, but I was simply wading through, waiting out my life. I went through the motions of living. I brushed my teeth and hair. I cooked meals for my mother and Carrol. I did housework and farm chores. I went to church each Sunday, and to the store each weekday. I was courteous and tried to be engaged with everyone around me, but there was always that extra layer in between me and the rest of the world.

Listening to Sam and Mr. Good greet each other, I realized I didn't feel quite like that anymore. Not when I was with Sam, riding home and talking to him, or sometimes not talking and just being in the quiet together. Something was different. I was different. Each time I was with Sam, pieces of that in-between layer were dissolving, bit by bit. I'd been so wrapped in the calm lift of how this change felt inside that I hadn't thought about anyone else noticing it on the outside.

Sam and I never really had any fancy dates. Our courtship was made up of our rides home each evening, and sometimes supper shared with my mother and Carrol at the farm. There was never any invitation for me to eat at the Purcell house, even after Sam had eaten with us several times. Sam explained that his mother didn't cook much or well, and his ravenous appreciation of the simple, filling meals in our kitchen proved it. By then it was winter, and there wasn't much of anywhere to go in Osceola Mills. The closest movie theater was in Madera, and we could have gone there, but somehow, we never did.

One night, I suggested going ice skating on Cooper's Pond, which was right at the edge of town by the brickworks. We had a pile of strap-on skates in our barn, and I wasn't a half-bad skater. Sam looked at me with such a pained expression that before he could reply I quickly said never mind, I didn't like skating much anyway. His relief was so big I could almost reach out and touch it. I had to swallow my giggle at the comical image of his long legs going in uncontrolled directions on the ice. Then I had to swallow the tears that came when I realized how renewed I felt by the simple, silly humor of that moment.

Several months passed in this easy rhythm. Sam stayed more and more often to eat with us. One night after supper, Sam and I took a walk down the lane between the house and the barn. That was the night I think our togetherness was sealed, made permanent in my heart and mind.

We'd had a mild, dripping day edged with coming spring, even though it was still only January. The house seemed stuffy after dinner. As Sam carried dishes from our long dining table to the sink in the kitchen, my mother shot me a knowing smile. It didn't go unnoticed that Sam always helped clear the table. Usually when my mother smiled like this, I pretended not to see her look, but this time I smiled back.

I grabbed Sam's hand and pulled him through the kitchen door before he could pull it away, and he didn't try to pull away. His grasp was firm and warm, and not a bit sweaty. Even after we were out the door, I didn't let go and neither did he. We simply started walking. I could just about match his pace, my stride long and his more loping.

We walked on past the barn, through the pasture and up onto the little rise overlooking the orchard. My breath released in frosty puffs ahead of me. It was colder out than it had seemed from inside the warm kitchen, but I was determined to hold on tight to the little bit of magic I felt pushing its way into my heart, pushing against the hardness there. Outside, the darkness enveloped us, allowing boldness. Now was the time to tell Sam about the baby, I decided. He needed to know, and I needed him to hear my story, my telling of it. I knew he must know some of it already, at least the basic facts. His kind patience and regard for me had kept him from asking me anything about that part of my young life, but I was ready to share it with him now.

"Sam, I want to tell you about my baby."

I began without any preamble. I didn't look at him as I spoke. I needed to focus on what I was pulling from deep inside. I gripped each black pearl of detail and freed it from its coiled strand. Sam stayed completely silent. I shivered as I spoke, more from the cold inside me than out. I did not talk about the birth, the pain, the pushing, the blood, the fear. Those are the graphic details men don't want to think much about, even though it's the way they themselves arrived, this fantastic and gory process of bringing new humans into the world. Those were not the important parts of my story then. I told Sam about what happened after the baby was born, of black emptiness, of guilt and regret. I explained as best I could that pieces of my heart were hard and untouchable still, and that I was afraid they might always stay that way.

Sam never let go of my hand as I talked. He looked at me as if he could see all the way through me to the hardness lodged inside, and see beauty there, too. He loved me truly. And I loved him, this quiet, stoic, slightly bumbling, very earnest man. I loved him in such a different way than I had loved before, calmer and less consuming than the way I had loved Holland. I trusted Sam with my heart, at least the pieces that were mine to offer.

Six

After Holland died in the hospital so swiftly, I'd felt like my life had been taken from me, too. Our life together and everything we'd had ahead of us had been pulled away and cast out into the realm of what would never be. What would take its place?

As my body ripened and my belly grew big, I sat for hours at a time in a big rocker on the wide wrapping porch of the farmhouse. Clear weather or foul, it made no difference. From the porch, I could see straight up into the beginnings of the Allegheny mountains. I saw threadbare hills, the weave of the earth showing through in all the places where the green of life had been worn away. Time fed continuously into itself in an endless loop. I must have slept. I must have eaten. I must have walked and talked and gone through the motions of each day, but my actions didn't connect to anything. I have few distinct memories of that time. I simply existed as my body went on with the work of nourishing a new living being.

During that blank and blackened time, my mother also waited. In its two-faced way, fate had decided we would be pregnant at the same time. In late winter, my youngest brother was born, my mother's last child. I didn't help with the birth as I had done before. I knew the baby was a boy, and I knew they named him Carrol. But I didn't really know him until much later.

When my own labor began, it shocked me viciously out of the in between with its first walloping pain. I stood in the kitchen, scraping carrots over the compost bucket we filled for the garden. I felt my insides drop out of me as a whoosh of watery release hit the kitchen floor. My body forced my attention, compelling me back down to earth from where I'd been suspended above. I was not as prepared as I really should have been for the intensity of the cramping pains that immediately knotted my insides. I gripped the side of the chopping block next to me, white-knuckled.

My mother had given birth to nine children, the last just a few months before, and she had survived it each time. Before it was my turn, I'd witnessed, more than once, the blood and pain and effort that colored in the lines of childbirth. I knew the mechanics involved in this passage from the warm, watery world of the womb into the bright, cold world outside. But I had no true idea of the pain. Amazingly, I hadn't suffered any of the usual childhood mishaps parceled out among my siblings and the other farm children we knew. No broken bones, fish-hooked fingers, felling illnesses. I'd always been very hardy, but this good fortune seemed less than lucky as I was twisted and wracked with contractions, stretched out of any shape resembling myself.

Each wave of pain came before I'd recovered from the last one. Every muscle contracted. Every nerve engaged. From somewhere far removed, my mother's voice told me to breathe, just breathe, as she led me to my bed, as she counted slow and steady, as she gripped my hand hard. I was knocked over, dragged under, tumbled around, consumed by the process that has existed since the beginning. Did it last minutes or hours or days? I didn't know time at all. My body lost its boundaries. The world roiled with pain and tears and my screams. In this most universal experience, I felt completely alone.

And then my mother, drenched in sweat and covered in my blood, handed me the slippery, squalling being who had been inside me moments before. A new life was here, and I was not alone any more. The grief and pain receded like a tide, and a new peace rushed over and through me, washing away everything else.

I named the baby Holland. It seemed the only choice. I hoped the name would bind him to the father he would never know as he went forward into the world. With my baby in the present, on the outside and needing me, I felt a purposeful leaning toward life again, a momentum that could carry me forward toward the day when this boy would smile at me, and then laugh, and then walk and talk.

Sadly, that feeling failed to carry me as far as I needed to go. It was like I'd reached the edge of a deep, deep pool. I had made it that far, and I hung on with grim determination, but that was the most I could manage. To desperately hang on. I couldn't haul myself out.

My mother couldn't, or wouldn't, help me. Was she afraid she would drown right along with me? She'd never had enough of a break after the birth of each child to let any swamping emotion take hold, be recognized, or given time to resolve. It's dreamlike, the memories of my mother telling me, imploring me, berating me, maybe for the simple reason that she just didn't know how to help me any other way.

"Louella, everyone goes through these things ... Louella, I'm sorry for you, but it's been enough time now ... Louella, we're all sorry that Holland is gone, but you have to think of the baby."

Her words pierced the layers of my immobility, but they weren't sharp enough to cut me free. Then she turned harder, callous in her frustration.

"Louella, do you think you're the only one who has ever lost a husband? Everyone dies."

Of course I knew that everyone died, and my mother had lost her share, but my heartache was beyond this logic. It was only a comment, one moment, but in that moment, I turned from her fully and sank deeper. Then my mother did what she must have thought was the only choice left, and my sister Angelica arrived.

Angelica was married to Arthur, the younger brother of one of the history teachers at the high school. Arthur had studied mechanical engineering at the state university, and when he graduated, he became a professor there. Angelica and Arthur lived in a large, new house in State College. They had a very comfortable life, but they didn't have any children. When my mother summoned Angelica after little Holland was born, my sister thrust herself into the middle of my suffering without hesitation. She recognized the chance to take from me something she desperately wanted.

To most people, the name Angelica sounds like *angelic*, but I'd always heard *jealous* in it. As a girl, Angelica was envious and unkind. When you live with so many siblings, you're bound to like some more than others, and I had always had a hard time liking Angelica. She was prettier, but I was smarter. Her envy of my quick mind made her find smug satisfaction in all my discomforts and failures.

A feeling of smallness and spite overlays all my memories of the children we were together. One summer day when I was six or seven, Lenore, Angelica, and I had taken ourselves down to the pond at the far end of the orchard after finishing our chores. The boys were already down there fishing, which they did often even though they never caught much of anything. The pond was small, but deep, shaded by the surrounding trees so that even in the heat of summer it was still cold. Its muddy, overgrown edges were alive with tadpoles and frogs. Turtles surfaced from its murky depths to warm themselves on available logs. I could spend hours watching these creatures, both their movements and their stillness. The flick of a frog's long tongue, the slow arch of a turtle's neck toward the sun. I squatted down to watch a bright green peeper make his way warily through the reeds. He eyed me the whole time, and I concentrated on not blinking. Marshall crept up behind me and pushed me hard, throwing me off balance and landing me face first in the water. I thrashed around, surprised and panicked and cold until I remembered that the water there was shallow enough for me to put my feet on the hidden bottom and stand up. It all happened in a matter of seconds. As I stood, shakily wiping hair and water out of my face, my eyes sought my sisters.

"Marshall, you idiot," Lenore said.

She moved to the edge of the pond and stretched out her hand to me. But Angelica didn't move a muscle. She just smirked, straightening her hair bow and smoothing her hands serenely down the front of her dry, unmuddied dress.

The baby was about two months old when Angelica made the half-day trip back to Osceola Mills, summoned by my mother. Even though I knew she was coming, I hadn't really registered the fact until I heard her on the stairs. I sat rocking Holland after nursing him to sleep. Angelica swished into the dim room. I knew it was her because my mother moved too briskly to swish that way. I kept my eyes closed and continued to rock. I felt like I never left that chair. I nursed, and then rocked and rocked to keep the baby asleep, and to keep myself comforted, too. The room was dark, the shades pulled against the light and the passing hours.

"Louella," Angelica said quietly as she sat in the straight chair next to mine.

I opened my eyes but did not reply. I had only seen Angelica once a year since she had married and moved away. Each time I saw her, I noticed a little more of her prettiness was gone. It must have been difficult to be a childless professor's wife, managing an empty household. She was not anyone's mother, and she was not an intellectual in that sea of learning. In the places where Angelica's beauty had worn away, the hard and petty bits of her nature showed clearly through.

"Louella," she said again, gesturing to my arms, "May I take him?"

And take him she did.

I sat up a little in the chair and handed the baby over without waking him. As Angelica lifted little Holland from my outstretched arms, a fresh softness overlaid the map of her face, and she was pretty once again. She wrapped her wiry body around my baby, and some of her bitterness evaporated. As Angelica held him, I felt lightened, unburdened, flooded with a surprising release.

Angelica looked at me with her eyes wide and shining. She explained that she knew for certain now there would be no baby of her own. She described how she wanted to provide this baby, my baby, with a comfortable home, a real education, and a father. And I agreed. In that moment, I agreed without hesitation to Angelica's description of a shining, complete life for this boy who deserved it, this innocent boy who did not deserve the kind of mother I was turning out to be.

I do believe now that Angelica and my mother thought they were helping me and doing what would be best for the baby. My sister desperately wanted to be a mother, and it was something her body couldn't accomplish. My body had produced a baby, but I couldn't seem to follow through. My mother assured me the baby would have a good, full life, that I would always know where he was and how he was, that I would be able to visit him, and Alden and Muriel would also. She did not go so far as to say I would still be his mother, but that seemed to make sense to me. Encouraged by her sense of purpose, and everyone else's apparent agreement, relief poured in and cemented itself around the broken fragments of everything else inside me.

Could my mother have remembered what it felt like to become a mother for the first time, to hold a first and only baby? Raising so many children, with the farm work and housework always mounting, and my father always badgering her, my mother had handed off many tasks, including babies, to her daughters, as soon as we could handle them. She couldn't have known, really, what it would do to me to let that one, that only one, go. Neither could she have predicted what was to happen.

Angelica left the following day. I didn't watch as she placed Holland's Moses basket on the seat of her shining new Model T, the top down in the early September sunshine. I did not see her add a carpet bag full of the baby's things next to the basket, smiling a bit smugly at my mother and Muriel, who had come to say goodbye. I did not watch as she cranked the motor, settled herself into the driver's seat, tied a scarf around her bright hair, and drove away. I sat in my chair, in the dim bedroom, rocking. I did not watch Angelica leave with my baby. But with my heart, I saw it all.

In the months that followed, I missed little Holland, but in a detached, unreal way. I loved him, but I'd been a mother to him for such a short, sad time. After a little while, my littlest brother, the baby Carrol, became like my own, but without any pain and loss attached. Having another baby in the household to tend to, even to marvel at, helped me reenter my existence bit by bit. I lived my life one hour at a time, then one day at a time, getting back into the rhythm of the farm, then going to work at the store for Mr. Good. I began to feel like I might get my footing again and be able to reconcile my old world with the new one, but I was wrong.

In the shelter of the complete and happy life I thought I'd given him over to, before I ever saw him again, little Holland contracted whooping cough. He died, and I lost him all over again.

My mother and Lenore traveled to State College for the quiet funeral service. I couldn't make myself go with them. Without any softness in her voice, my mother told me I would regret this, my inability to face facts, my denial. But it wasn't denial that made me immobile. It was bottomless grief, and I could only deal with it by sinking deeper into myself right where I was. I had failed at being a mother and given my baby away. Angelica had failed at being a mother and had let him die. Had he really belonged to either one of us?

That was the endpoint of the story I told Sam that night on the chilled rise overlooking the orchard. Those were the details that for so many years I'd seen as the endpoint of my story, too. As we stood there together, Sam and I, and the dark around us grew deeper, I looked up into the star sequined sky and lost myself in it, lost any feeling of separateness between my body and the universe. My sadness and loss seemed to unfurl from within me, dissolving into the blackness of that night.

After that night, I reminded myself many times over how fortunate I really was in spite of my losses. Each time Sam reached for my hand, each time he pulled me close with his warm grasp around my waist, I thought about how many different kinds of love there were in the world.

When I had married the first time, I'd considered myself grown up. I hadn't known how much growing up I still had to do. I had no idea how fast it would happen,

and how much of it would be forced by loss. I had loved
Holland surely with an innocent, untested spirit. Then
the death of my young husband had been followed so
swiftly by the gain of a baby, miraculous and
overwhelming. Then I'd lost him, too. I still loved him, so
many years later, that tiny being who had been my son,
but I'd kept that love locked tight away so it wouldn't
break me.

Now I had this new kind of love with Sam, a
different kind of love again. Our love was a respite, a
haven. It was a feeling and a place I didn't know could
exist for me in all the years I had spent as a widow, as the
mother of a dead child. I began to realize that my story of
losing Holland and then my baby, and in the process also
losing myself, would not have to be my whole story after
all.

Seven

In the spring, the nights turned warm, the world turned green, and Sam proposed to me. As the fall and winter months had passed, he'd learned to trust in himself the things I already trusted in him, to believe I loved him for what his steady love gave me, and for the man he was independent of my love.

The evening he asked me to marry him started out like most others we'd shared. Sam picked me up at the store, and we drove toward home. He seemed like himself, maybe just a little quieter than usual, but I didn't sense anything too different until he pulled over to the side of the road just before we reached the farm.

It didn't take me completely by surprise, this roadside proposal. I had expected Sam would ask me to marry him at some point soon, and I didn't expect anything romantic or elaborate. We were older, and it was wartime. Sam wasn't fancy, and neither was I.

He didn't say a word until he was out of the car and opening my door. He helped me out, and when I saw that he was about to get down on his knee, I stopped him because the grass by the side of the road was muddy. He pulled a red velvet ring box from his pocket, opened it, and held it out in between us in offering. The ring itself did surprise me. Most women I knew didn't have engagement rings. I'd thought we would just choose simple bands for our marriage ceremony, but instead, nestled in the box was a diamond ring, delicate and definite at the same time. Where had Sam gotten such a ring or the idea that I needed one? It was beautiful. It was just right.

We told my mother and Carrol we were engaged as soon as we got to the farm. I didn't want to shed the deep, enveloping happiness of the moment at the door, and I knew my mother had been expecting this development anyway. I walked into the kitchen on light feet, and Sam walked in behind me with confidence. He knew my mother would be happy and would welcome him. She hugged me then. She was not usually much of a hugger, and when she drew me close that night, I felt an easing in her careworn body.

"Welcome to the family," said Carrol, shaking Sam's hand firmly. With that phrase, my little brother seemed all too grown up.

Sam stayed for supper that night, and my mother chattered on uncharacteristically about how nice a spring wedding would be, and where we might live, and how we had never really had a college man in the family, Arthur forgotten in all her enthusiasm. She didn't pause long enough for the rest of us to comment much. Her talk filled in the gaps between her relief that this had finally happened and her disbelief that it had. Carrol didn't say much, beyond nodding and "mhhming," but he smiled at me a lot.

After dinner, I walked back out to the car with Sam, wanting a few more minutes, wishing this next part of our lives could start right away that night. As we stood by the open car door, he tested the idea of telling his own mother about our engagement.

"I'd like you to be with me. We should really tell her together," he said, raising his eyebrows a fraction. His statement was both tentative and resolute.

"I already told her I was going to ask you. She didn't really say much one way or the other."

That figured. I wasn't surprised much. Unresponsiveness would have been Willetta's backhand way of daring him to truly do it. I had so far avoided much direct contact with Sam's mother, but what I'd had was enough to confirm what I thought I'd known about her all along. Mrs. Purcell was the kind of woman who took pleasure in playing the role of the elderly widow, someone to be respected and served. She was detached and disinterested, but at the same time I was pretty sure she also viewed herself as vital to the livelihood of our small community.

Sundays were Sam's designated time with Willetta. We usually saw each other at church, but Sam had never suggested that I spend any other part of a Sunday together with them. Sam walked this fine line very diplomatically. He always sat with his mother in their usual front pew, and then he would seek me out after the service to say hello and goodbye at the same time, before they went home to their dinner. Willetta would trail majestically behind him once they were outside the church, nodding or giving a brief greeting to anybody who greeted her. She was so clearly above them, those poor, less fortunate souls. She was very tall, taller than me by a few inches, so she was above most of them, literally. I think she believed her attitude was elegant, but to everyone around her it was just plain cold.

On those Sundays after church, when she reached the place where Sam and I stood talking, she would nod at me, and then at my mother and Carrol.

"Louella, Carrol, Mrs. Reams."

She never used my mother's given name, which was Alma. Sometimes she would stand with us for a minute or two and make a comment about the weather or the sermon. Never an inquiry. Never anything personal. Never anything about Sam and me. After that, she would simply move on toward Sam's car. She would stand by the passenger door with her lips pursed until Sam caught up and opened the door for her. Then he would wait for her to settle herself and close the door gently after her. By this time, I knew him well enough to sense his internal eye roll, his inside grin.

So, as we stood outside the night of our engagement saying goodbye, and Sam assured me his mother would be different if we were together telling her our news officially, I wasn't so sure. Neither could Sam have been, really. I knew Sam was right that we should tell his mother together, we should present a united front. I was uncomfortable, but not unwilling. It wasn't right or fair that Sam had to control for his mother's sourness and disappointment, but I knew it was accurate. She didn't want him to get married and leave her. She certainly didn't want him to marry an older woman who had already been married, who had given birth to a child. To Willetta, I was scarred and used up, certainly not good enough for a Purcell.

Shouldn't good enough be measured in the amount of happiness and love to be found? Shouldn't a mother simply want that comfort and companionship for her child? But how was I really to know? I was no one's mother anymore, after all.

In that spring of 1944, the only other news continued to be war news. Our town and all the towns around it had been pretty much empty of young men since the bombing of Pearl Harbor. Sam had registered for the draft in 1940. Even then, the United States anticipated certain involvement in the war. It was a when, not an if. Sam's draft number had not come up so far, but, as so many men did, he wanted to join up anyway, driven by that instinct to take action and be part of it all. He'd only held off because of his mother's insistence.

Once Sam and I found each other, though, I think as much changed inside him as it did inside of me, and he didn't feel it was right to wait any longer. He decided to enlist in the Army Signal Corps, based at Fort Monmouth, New Jersey. It was done in a matter of minutes, the day after we decided to get married. Through the uncomplicated process of entering the enlistment office in Philipsburg, going through a basic physical, and signing his name to the dotted line, Sam committed us to a new life in a new place. Just like that.

When Sam came to the store the following night to get me, I was ready for him to tell me all the details of his enlistment. Instead he picked up the subject of his mother just where we'd left off the night before, suggesting I go home with them after church that coming Sunday. He said we could tell his mother about our plans at dinner, and then it would be over and done with.

"It won't be that bad, you know. She is my mother."

I thought maybe I'd wounded him a little with my lack of enthusiasm. Whether she was kind or not, whether she would be thrilled at our news or not, Sam was trying to do the right thing, to be a good son. I resolved that I would not make it harder than it needed to be, would not voice every hesitation. I put on a broad, loving smile and told him of course I would come to dinner on Sunday.

"I didn't tell her I enlisted yet, either," he added while I was still smiling.

I smiled wider. "Well, I hope she's ready for a slap, bang, wallop."

This was my mother's most frequent expression in dire circumstances. I took a deep breath. Sam and I were getting married and moving away. Nothing was going to change that. He was in my corner, and I was in his. I hoped that would be the shape of our marriage always.

The Sunday dinner with Sam's mother came and went about how I expected, and we survived it. Willetta said, "I see," and "well," too many times for me to count, and she didn't say too much beyond that. She didn't ask us about the details of our wedding plans. She didn't ask for any specifics about Sam's enlistment or the fact that it would mean we'd be moving away. She didn't treat our news as any cause for celebration. For her, it wasn't.

I smiled and tried to be pleasant, but I refused to fill in the gaps with empty chatter. I had vowed to myself to keep calm, to not get riled or give over anything to make me seem weak. Despite all the long silences, I wasn't downcast or discouraged. I saw for sure that the husband I'd signed up for would be the one who showed up, whatever the circumstances. Willetta's disdain and her dismissal, her refusal to share in our happiness, did not seem to make Sam angry or upset. He was used to her. He didn't cajole her, and he didn't cower or apologize. Throughout that afternoon and evening, he remained the same quiet, steady man I knew and loved.

As we stood in the hall to say goodbye after dinner, I grasped Willetta's hand and held it firmly for a moment. She looked alarmed as I looked her straight in the eye.

"Mrs. Purcell," I said resolutely and with what I hoped seemed a genuine smile. "I love Sam very much, and I'm going to be as good a wife to him as I can. I know you love him very much, too, so I hope it will make you happy to know how happy I am going to make him. Thank you for dinner."

When I let go of her hand, it remained upraised, as if still in my grasp. I allowed myself a small triumph at the look of shock on her face.

Eight

The next chapter of our lives began, and I was ready. Had I ever thought I would be at this kind of beginning again? Sam would have to go through basic training at Fort Jackson in South Carolina before reporting to Fort Monmouth for Signal Corps Training School. After he finished up basic training, we would get married and move to Fort Monmouth. With our plan in place, I woke up every morning feeling buoyant, purposeful. It always took me a minute to come fully awake and remember the reason. That's right, I was getting married!

Even though Fort Monmouth wasn't far in miles, it was farther in spirit than anyone in my family had ever gone. Holland and I had taken day trips close to home sometimes, mostly to visit my brothers and sisters in towns almost interchangeable with ours, but I had never been to Philadelphia. I had never left Pennsylvania. I had never seen an ocean. Osceola Mills, our farm, my mother, and my brother would all still be right there where they'd always been, and I would hold them all in my heart, but they would hold themselves together just fine without me.

While Sam was at Fort Jackson, he wrote me letters almost every day. The letters were Sam on paper, but they were also something more. More reflective, braver, funnier. One entire letter read just like this:

Dearest Louella – Nothing new, nothing to do, love from me to you. – Sam

I smiled over this one for three days straight until the next letter arrived, longer and more descriptive. In it Sam told me about the other men in his barracks, about the commanders, and all the drilling and marching. He told me that the overcast weather was grey to the point of tears, but that the fierce mosquitoes seemed to be steering clear of him most of the time. He said the free hours were harder to get through than the scheduled ones, because that was when he had time to think about how much he couldn't wait to see me again.

There was no fear in Sam's words. He didn't write about if and when he might be somewhere much farther away than South Carolina. Sam was careful not to seem too eager, but I could tell a piece of him was poised to prove his mettle. *Soldier* was a badge of masculinity to pin to the uniform of this whole new life. I missed him, but I had practice at being alone, and this new aloneness was so much easier for me. It was trimmed with hope instead of resignation and loss.

In Sam's last letter from Fort Jackson he explained that before returning to Pennsylvania he would need to report to Fort Monmouth. He'd been encouraged to apply for the accelerated wartime Officer Candidate School there, which meant some extra paperwork. Then he would have a short leave to drive back to Osceola, get married, collect his household possessions, and transport wife and goods back to New Jersey. I read this letter over and over. The word *wife* chimed in my head and sent warmth all the way through me.

Our wedding was as we were, uncomplicated and straightforward. We were married in the Osceola Mills Methodist church where Holland and I had also been married. Many years later, the details of the day I married Sam would fade away. The flowers decorating the sanctuary, the piano music, the new dress I wore, the small gathering of our guests. All these things would become lovely, blurred background. What remained precise was the look in Sam's eyes as I walked through the wide double doors at the back of the church and down the aisle toward him. His expression remained serious, but his eyes were filled with true, unguarded joy and relief. I was feeling all those same things, and I lost myself in his look. Being married in the same place where I had already been married once before felt more right than wrong, as if my life were connecting and coming full circle. I was certainly not the only woman to get married more than once in this same church. Widows were not rare. The lucky ones found someone else to love, or at least found companionship. On that day, I could finally, truly count myself among the lucky ones.

Nine

Sam was accepted into the Officer Candidate School program, and while he completed his training, the Army would provide us with housing in an apartment building on the base. I was looking forward to creating a home of my own, even if it was a collection of rooms within shared walls. In my whole life so far, I had only gone from living on my family's farm as a daughter to Holland's family's farm as a wife and then right back again. I'd never made my own nest. Our nest would be small, but in the best way, a contained, precise, purposeful space.

After all the packing up and the goodbyes, we'd had a long drive from Pennsylvania. I was ready to stop moving and start making my home, but Sam drove us first to the beach. Fort Monmouth was only five miles from the ocean, the ocean I'd never seen. Now Sam wanted me to see it first thing.

The June evening was warm but windy, and the beach parking lot was empty when we pulled in. The sand made a gritty vibration under the tires after miles and miles of mostly smooth road. Sam stopped the car, we both got out, and I laughed as we stretched skyward at exactly the same time.

"Take your shoes off," Sam urged, as he took his own shoes off and then peeled off his black socks.

I hesitated for a small second. Then I took my shoes off too, and rolled my cotton stockings down and away from my feet. We left our shoes neatly paired and lined up like sentinels on the strip of pavement in front of the car. The sand was cool and dry, falling away beneath my bare toes. It wasn't at all like the farm dirt my feet had always known. Sam stood at the top of the sloping beach, hands on hips, completely straight and upright, like some invisible weight had been lifted off his shoulders by this arrival. He looked at ease and in charge, brim full of confidence.

I left him there satisfied and walked ahead, sinking a little into the sand with each step. When I got to the water's edge, the sea swirled around my feet, beckoning and sucking and rolling away into endlessness. There, with that ocean vastness in front of me, I felt sure life went far beyond what we could see and touch and know. I felt that each of us does not begin and end in aloneness as it so often seems. We go on and on together in an enduring, fused cycle.

My feet were still sandy inside my stockings as we left the parking lot, carrying a little bit of the beach away with me. When we turned into the entrance at Fort Monmouth, we stopped to show Sam's identification and assignment papers to the two privates stationed at the gate. I was surprised by a surge of protectiveness and a rush of homesickness as they greeted us. They looked so much like young boys playing soldier, standing there in all their seriousness. They reminded me of Carrol. I felt sharply out of place in that moment, as these boys in uniform saluted us. Then we were waved through, swallowed into whatever our new life would be.

As Sam drove us on, every turn looked the same to me, each squared street pivoting precisely onto the next. The whole complex seemed calm, quieter than I had imagined. It was almost night by then, the light leaching from a pink and orange sky. Maybe here, just like in any other town or neighborhood, life at this hour reverted inward and slowed down.

Finally, we arrived at the end of Hickory Lane, where our building stood. An alley divided two pairs of brick apartment houses that made up the officer candidate housing area. A bay of garages sat at the end of the alley in between, and one large door was still open, ready and waiting for us. We decided to bring in just what we needed for that night and leave everything else in the car for unpacking the next day.

Sam opened the trunk and took out our two maroon suitcases. They were a gift from Sam's mother, ordered from the Sears catalog after he told her he had enlisted. Willetta was very clear that the luggage was not an engagement gift, and that distinction had made it even more satisfying to pack my clothing into one of the suitcases.

I led the way through the narrow alley, and Sam followed with the suitcases. I heard voices floating to me from somewhere nearby, attached to bodies I couldn't see. More than two, it sounded like a group of four or five in conversation. As we turned the corner around to the front of our building, the sharp bark of a man's laugh was followed by women's softer answering ones, and then they all melted together, low and harmonious.

Our building had double front doors, each entrance leading to two apartments. Ours was number 201, on the second floor. The building was new, the stairs solid and quiet as I climbed. Following right behind me, Sam set down the suitcases outside the door at the top of the stairs. He looked at me expectantly. We'd been told at the guard booth that Sam could pick up our keys the next day from his Commanding Officer. The apartment would be unlocked for our arrival. As I reached for the door knob, Sam grabbed my hand. He swung my arm up around his shoulder and over his neck, and he scooped me up. He did it all in one motion before I could even start to protest.

"I think I'm supposed to carry you inside, Mrs. Purcell," he said, grinning in this rare moment of romanticism.

He reached for the door knob from underneath my legs, turned it, and then gently kicked the door open. With that, Sam carried me ceremoniously over the threshold of our first home. It was not until hours later that we remembered our suitcases, still waiting patiently in the little hallway outside our door.

Ten

I woke up early the next morning. Birdsong and weak sunlight spilled in through our bare bedroom window, cracked open to let in the breeze. I breathed in slowly, and out again. I didn't feel as displaced as I'd expected. Even though this apartment was not home yet in a truly known way, I felt like I was just where I was supposed to be. When I turned over to face Sam, he was already awake, too. He smiled at me, pulled me in close to him for a moment, and then suggested we go find some breakfast in town before he had to report.

After breakfast, Sam went to meet with his Commanding Officer, and I set off to find my way around our new world. I decided to go to the commissary first. I spent a fascinating and slightly bewildering two hours wandering in the wilds of the Fort Monmouth commissary, which was so much bigger, newer, and more spread out than Wallace Good's store. I'd walked up and down each aisle deliberately, deciding on everything I wanted to buy when Sam and I came back together in the evening. I had been too wonderstruck to even remember to buy myself something for lunch.

By the time I returned to the apartment house, it seemed like I'd been trekking for days, but it wasn't even lunchtime yet. When I reached the top of the stairs, I saw a piece of paper fixed to our door with a little strip of masking tape.

Welcome from your neighbor downstairs in number 101! I'm looking forward to meeting you. Please come down for some refreshments when you have time. Yours, Natalie Haworth

A nervous ripple pushed through me as I read the note. I knew I couldn't pretend I hadn't read it, hadn't seen it. I would have to act on this invitation and go downstairs. It had been a long time since I'd met someone new, one on one. I wasn't counting Sam. Had I ever, as an adult, truly made a new friend? Oh, Louella, she's a neighbor being friendly, offering iced tea or something, I told myself, but my uneasiness tapped the root of something deeper, something I hadn't allowed myself to think about during the excitement and activity of getting married and packing up.

I'd been so ready to move here with Sam and start our new life, but even so, now that we'd arrived, I had to admit how untested I really was. I was basically unfamiliar with the workings of the wider world. I'd disentangled and detached myself from all the threads of belonging that had tethered me to one place my whole life. I'd done so purposely, with intent, but all the newness was still daunting. In Osceola, almost all the people I'd encountered in my everyday life were the same people I'd known since childhood. They knew me, my family, my story, my griefs, and I knew theirs. Those attachments had been forged by circumstance, not by choice.

Now, for the first time after forty years of life, I wasn't sure who I was, who I wanted to be in this new life I'd chosen. I didn't want to misstep, to say or do anything to define this new self on the outside while I was still figuring out who this new woman was on the inside. I wasn't the Pennsylvania Louella Reams I had always been. Who would I be now that I was Louella Purcell in New Jersey? I thought about how choice and circumstance danced with each other, really part of one circle twining around us and then spinning out away from us again.

I decided to go meet Natalie right then, before I could change my mind, before I could think any further about the deeper meaning of every step, every hello. Maybe hers was one of the voices I'd heard outside the night before. That gentle, easy laughter in the twilight had sounded genuine and at home.

I went back down the steps I had just come up. The door to the downstairs apartment had a bright, silk-flowered wreath hanging just below the number. I would never have thought to put a wreath on an inside door, or on any door really, other than at Christmastime. We'd always made Christmas wreaths for the outside doors on the farm, using boughs and sprigs from our own pine trees. The needles stung our chilled hands, and the sap made our fingers almost too sticky for the job. I didn't know whether to think a flowered wreath inside on an apartment door was a pretty touch, or pointless. I pictured the type of Natalie who might hang that kind of wreath. She had long, blond, Veronica Lake curls and a broad, red lipstick smile. She wore a pink shirtwaist flaring out from a tiny middle, and slightly impractical black pumps.

I raised my hand and knocked just above the wreath, and the woman who opened the door did not match my image at all. She was young, maybe twenty years younger than I was. She wore a flouncy yellow and red apron tied over men's grey trousers, and a loose, button down blue shirt.

"You got my note? I'm Natalie Haworth," she said.

She had a sincere smile, no lipstick. Her hair was shortish, practical, and dark brown.

I decided then that I liked her wreath.

"Yes, thank you. I'm Louella Purcell." My new name felt unusual when I said it, but in a good way, like the feel of a summer's first ice cream cone.

"It's so nice to meet you. Come in."

I followed Natalie through the door, and stood for a minute looking around the apartment, which was laid out the same as ours upstairs. It was one big room arranged into separate areas for cooking, eating, and everything else, with what I was sure were two bedrooms and a bathroom off a short hallway opposite the living area. A baby girl, about a year old, sat in a high chair pulled up to one end of the dining table.

"Please sit down," Natalie said, nodding toward the table. "That's Susan."

Susan eyed me intently while Natalie disappeared into the kitchen area. She came back out with a tray holding a pitcher of iced tea and two glasses, which she unloaded onto the table. The baby shifted her watch from me to her mother. Natalie went back into the kitchen and when she came out this time the tray held napkins, little plates, a basket of what looked like banana bread, and a bowl of grapes.

I sat down opposite the baby, and Natalie sat down across from me, next to the high chair. She smiled at her little daughter. The little girl smiled back, a wide baby grin revealing the pearly bits of four front teeth. When I had thought about meeting new people once Sam and I moved, I hadn't thought much about the children who would come along with them. There had been lots of mothers and children at the commissary that morning, but they had just been bodies on the outskirts of my attention then. This was different.

"Susan is our only one, so far. Do you have any children? Where did you move from? What is your husband's name?"

I must have looked wide-eyed as I took in all these questions at once, not sure which to answer first, because Natalie laughed and then apologized. This made me laugh too, and then the baby laughed, and I felt my face relax a little bit.

"No, we don't have any children."

I paused just a breath. Then I went on.

"My husband is Sam, and we moved here from Osceola Mills, Pennsylvania."

I'd answered all her questions, though not in order. I didn't think it mattered.

"We've just gotten married. Just two days ago, in fact," I added.

"Congratulations! That's wonderful," Natalie said with another broad smile.

I could tell she did think it was wonderful, and she didn't seem surprised that I had no children and had only just gotten married. It was wartime, after all, and the patterns and sequences of regular life were rearranged for almost everyone. She couldn't know that the irregular pattern of my life had nothing to do with the war, that my details had been rearranged long ago.

We chatted about this and that, smiling every time the baby smiled, or smashed food into her mouth, the little pieces of bread and cheese becoming unrecognizable mush in her tight fists. We smiled, too, when she wailed and screeched at being unable to pick up more chunks of bread and cheese once her fingers were gummed together.

When I got up to leave and noticed the clock hanging by the front door, I saw that I'd been there for over an hour. It had seemed like ten minutes. Natalie said it was the baby's naptime, and she herself might lie down for a bit, too. As she stood, I saw the slight swell of her abdomen. I had missed it before, hidden beneath her apron. Natalie said she was so happy I had come down to visit, and she was sure we would see each other all the time now that we were neighbors.

I agreed and thanked her. As I went back up the stairs to my own apartment, I sorted out my thoughts. Natalie seemed so at ease, so young and untouched, but I knew that everything about someone else's life did not usually lie right at the surface for all to see. Young or not, she was sincere, and I thought she would be a good neighbor to have. And I had endured an hour of new friendship.

Sam's officer candidate program included some classroom time and a lot of practical training hours. He was gone overnight a lot to other parts of New Jersey and even to New York City. While he was gone, Sam wrote me letters again. He couldn't include many details of what he was doing for the Army, so instead he filled his letters with other things. He wrote about going to the Roxy Theater and the Empire State Building, about how no one in a uniform was charged admission anywhere. He described how strangely dark and deserted the big city seemed. His favorite closing, *Yours to have and to hold until the cows come home*, always made me smile, because of course it would have been much more appropriate if we'd been back in Pennsylvania.

I was alone while Sam was gone, but I wasn't lonely, which was so opposite to the way things had been. Before I married Sam, I had been lonely, even though I was almost never alone.

Before we'd left, Sam's mother gave me her Singer sewing machine. New machines weren't available during the war because the Singer factories had been converted for government use, but Willetta's machine was barely used, and I was happy to take it. Sam's father had given it to her as an anniversary gift not long after Sam was born, but Sam said he'd never once seen his mother use it. Willetta never took to sewing, and she didn't need to, either. The Purcells could always afford store bought clothes and whatever household things they wanted.

In the weeks before our wedding, I'd sorted through my mother's fabrics, claiming pieces I had always liked. Then the Goods invited me to choose whatever fabrics I wanted from the store as a wedding gift. All in all, as we pulled away from town on the June morning following our wedding, I think the fabric took up more room than all our other things combined.

When Sam was gone off the base, I spent my hours making curtains, tablecloths, and slipcovers to warm the apartment up and make it feel like ours. With my sewing machine and my new husband's letters to entertain me, I didn't even realize how much I'd really been missing Sam until he was back again from New York at the end of July. He told me he was officially finished with his training. He would begin his real work with the Signal Corps and wouldn't need to leave again for a while. We fell into an easy rhythm of days apart and evenings back together again, as easy as the habit of rides home along a cold country road that had first brought us together.

Eleven

The summer months at Fort Monmouth flowed smoothly into autumn, and then almost before I knew it, it was Christmastime. Sam and I had celebrated Christmases together in Pennsylvania before we were married, but our first New Jersey Christmas felt more official.

It was unlike any Christmas I'd experienced before. The Army base was overwhelmed with festiveness, even though it was wartime, or maybe because of it. I didn't have to make my own Christmas wreaths that year. The boys from the local Boy Scout troop came door-to-door around the base, singing carols and selling wreaths as part of the war effort. Their earnestness was greater than their musical talent by far, but I don't think a single wife on the base said no to a wreath. By the end of the first week in December, almost every door at Fort Monmouth, inside and out, was decorated with a Boy Scout wreath. All of them were lopsided, with drooping red bows and sprigs sticking out here and there, but we hung them with pride.

On Christmas Eve, Sam and I went to a midnight candlelight service of carols, something else I had never done before. The Methodist service in Osceola had always been on Christmas morning. The church would be filled with tired men who had worked extra hours at the brickyard or the railroad the day before, or who had been up for hours already because a farm didn't take care of itself, even on Christmas Day. The women were impatient, anxious to get home and start getting the holiday meal ready for their large families. The rambunctious children didn't want to sit still for one minute longer than necessary, ready to plunge down the sledding hills and devour candy canes on one of the few days when chores were lightened.

In comparison, on that first Christmas Eve in New Jersey, the come-one, come-all Army church was filled to standing room only with smiling, expectant people. Wrapped around us all was a warm, dense joy, like something alive I could almost throw my arms around. Dozens of white candles flickered on the windowsills of the long, narrow sanctuary, making each window glow from beneath. As I looked all around in that darkness, I realized how many of the faces were familiar to me now, when six months before they had all belonged to strangers. I felt like I belonged there. The curtain had been lifted, the in-between layer pulled back. Life and my understanding of it in this new place was a gift. For the first time I felt connected to the real meaning of this holiday I'd been celebrating for so many years.

Our Christmas felt over, though, when Sam told me he would be gone again for six weeks right after the New Year. He left on January third, and once he was gone, our apartment was more empty and my heart less content than all the other times he'd been away.

Sam was one of only five officers chosen for a special detached assignment, and I knew he was quietly proud of this selection, of using his talents and knowledge in a vital way to serve his country. His letters this time around came with a return address of the New York City Defense Recreation Committee on Park Avenue. Even though I knew it was just a pass through, reading that address on each envelope filled me with patriotic pride, too. Alongside my pride was a great relief that Sam was writing from New York and not France, or even farther, a relief in brains over brawn. If Sam continued to be selected for special assignments, he might not end up overseas at all. I tried to imagine how I would feel if he were really shipping out, but the thought served no purpose, so I pulled back from it and tied it up in a separate place. I was well practiced at this.

Twelve

Sam had been gone four weeks into the new year when I knew for certain I was pregnant. Even though my body had done this once before, it had been so, so long ago. I really hadn't thought much about babies at all since marrying Sam. I was just so surprised and then happy to be part of a well-matched pair. I never allowed for the idea that we could expand beyond that contentment. I'd pushed the idea of children into the far corners of my mind, knowing I was probably too old. Knowing I had already failed once. Sam had never talked about children either. I think he'd considered parenthood a closed subject. But, yes, I was pregnant, at the beginning of something else new. As much as I thought I understood Sam so far, what he'd think of this development, I truly did not know.

Sam arrived back at Fort Monmouth on February 14, 1945. Valentine's Day, appropriately. He didn't warn me he was coming, and I was surprised by a knock at the door in the middle of the afternoon.

"Who is it?" I called out with half attention as I sat at the sewing machine.

"Louella?" he said in answer.

That was all he said. Then I was flinging the door wide, and his lanky frame was filling all the open space. He smelled of cold, wet wool. He was home, and I felt the comfort of it flood through me, even though I'd known all along he wasn't too far away, wasn't really in danger, and was coming back. My reaction must have been instinct, compounded and sharpened by my present pregnant state. I was in his arms before I knew it.

And then I drew back, scalded by a hot realization. I hadn't been thinking about how I was going to tell Sam about the baby. I hadn't known to be prepared quite yet, today, but here he was, and I was not good at waiting to share news now that I had this man to share it with. I couldn't, wouldn't, allow myself to think at all about the last time I'd had this news to share with a husband. I regained my breath. Sam looked me up and down, and grinned boyishly, a rare look for him. While he smiled at me, I plunged.

"I'm pregnant."

He didn't reply.

"Sam, did you hear me?" I demanded.

Because he stood, staring at me, totally silent, completely stilled. He had almost returned to the dumbstruck state he'd been in the first night I had accepted a ride home, and I was momentarily thrown off balance, thrown back. *Oh, where was I? What was I doing here? Who was this man?* But then Sam recovered. His face rearranged itself into a look of unrestrained joy. We had never talked about it, we had never expected it, but I knew in that instant that my husband had wanted this with his whole heart.

Throughout that pregnant spring and summer, I spent many hours pleading with the heavy air to shift as I sat directly in front of the big gunmetal fan in our bedroom. The extra person inside me created a new heat, making that New Jersey summer feel so different from all the Pennsylvania summers I'd known.

My first experience with motherhood had been so searing, and after that I'd felt like the part of me designed to be someone's mother was had been sealed over, made inaccessible. Sometimes I woke up in the middle of the night uncomfortable, short of breath or struggling to turn over. In my half sleep I was puzzled. Then I remembered, and in the dark I would be filled with the shining light of this unexpected gift. But my losses were there too, a small shadow. In those quiet hours, I turned my hope and my worries over again and again. They were like pieces of sea glass tumbled in the ever-shifting ocean. Sometimes they came up clean in my palm, edges softened, the remnants of my sadness buffed away. Sometimes. And that was all I could expect.

One awful, stifling afternoon in August, I tried to nap and failed. I moved outside to the front steps of the apartment building, just for the change of scene. I knew it wouldn't really be any cooler out there. I was glad to find the space empty of neighbors or company at least.

I'd been crocheting a blanket for the baby for a few months, and I had it draped over my lap as I sat on the steps. It was much too hot, but I needed something to do with my hands, which were always restless despite my general sluggishness. That afternoon, out in the daytime light, I realized in sort of a sudden way that the design of the blanket was not right for a baby at all. It was bright and chunky, with garish roses crocheted into the middle of each glaring white square. What had I been thinking? I must have chosen it for its happy and cheerful pattern, because I was happy, in a more substantial way than I had been for a long, long time. *And whatever was wrong with that?* Then the moment I gave myself that reason, it was whisked away from me. I couldn't snatch it back fast enough. The bottom dropped out, and I was breathless, overcome with heaving sobs, the shards of my past slicing me open again.

Sam found me this way, immobilized, my lap covered in my half-finished work, hands twisted in the white wool. The evening had begun to cool just slightly, the turning of autumn hovering above us. He sat down beside me on the top step. He didn't say anything, but he untangled my hands and wrapped them together in both of his. I thought I had used all my available tears, but the sweetness of this man whose heart spoke to mine even as his voice remained still made me cry all over again for my good fortune. I cried in gratitude for the peace that settled on me whenever Sam was near.

Thirteen

Margaret Lenore was born on September 7, 1945, just after my forty-second birthday. Sam bought a new camera the day before she was born. As he snapped the first pictures of Margaret and me, he smiled and teased me that I didn't look a day over forty.

We could have named our daughter after one of our mothers or used another family name, but I wanted something unattached, unencumbered. I wanted a name new to my heart. We'd already chosen *Lenore* as a middle name, after my favorite sister, but I considered deeply which name would be just right for a first. *Margaret* is an old name. It means *pearl*. Both *Margaret* and *pearl* sounded both pretty and strong to me, feminine and definite at the same time. When I chose *Margaret*, I chose it for its strength, for the *grit* that grounded its sound, the grit that I knew a daughter would need to face the world. As she grew, I would come to realize the meaning of Margaret's name was even more fitting than I'd first thought. A pearl is precious but opaque. There's no seeing the inside of a pearl. Similarly, the insides of Margaret's heart and mind were often unknowable to me.

Margaret was a joy and a challenge all at the same time. Compared to the newness and delicateness of her tiny body, her personality seemed fixed and intense right from the start. She was generally quiet, but with an almost wry smile and a discerning glint in her eye that made me think she'd been around this world at least once already.

Being needed by this baby brought me out of myself even more than marriage and moving had. When Margaret was born, I emerged. With a baby in my arms, I felt more purposeful. Now I had an obvious, tangible reason for being. Margaret's sunshine and her squalling filled my heart and stretched it into a new shape, pushing strenuously and constantly against the barricades I'd made there. I felt my earlier loss keenly alongside this new love, but I didn't feel undone by it. The plain truth was that I would never, could never, have had the gift of this baby without losing the other one first.

The war in Europe had officially ended on May 8, 1945, with the surrender of all German troops, but it felt more truly over when the Japanese agreed to sign the documents of surrender in September following the destruction of Hiroshima and Nagasaki. This was just days before Margaret was born. When my child joined the outside world, it was a world at peace, at least on paper. I was relieved, but my relief was paralleled by the horror of knowing how many Japanese mothers and children had perished in that last worst push toward victory. Peace was made brittle by the tandem grief of so many mothers whose children were lost and gone, whose children who would never grow up or grow old. I knew this vast, deep sorrow all too well.

When Margaret was a month old, we arranged to have her baptized by the minister at the Fort Monmouth church. We were not regular church goers, and I worried that the minister would question us pointedly about this, about our faith and our intent. That would have been his right. But Army life is different from civilian life in so many ways, wartime and its aftermath so different from ordinary time. At Fort Monmouth, everyone came and went irregularly, everyone was from somewhere else. The minister, Reverend Robison, looked smilingly at Margaret as we sat in his office to discuss the service. He assured us that he would be honored to christen our daughter as a precious new addition to the Fort Monmouth family.

The late October morning of Margaret's baptism broke clear and blue. The crisp beauty of the day was only on the edges of my awareness. Margaret was quietly asleep in my arms, and I focused all my energy on keeping her that way. What if she woke up and cried? What if she was hungry? What if she spit up all over? When Sam and I moved toward the front of the sanctuary where we'd been asked to sit, I saw other mothers with babies in their arms or small children by their sides, but Margaret was the only one being baptized, the only one who would be front and center.

Just like all those Christmas services in Osceola, I'd also attended countless baptisms there. I'd never really thought about what they meant, beyond tradition, the ritual of enfolding each new baby into the life of the church and the life of our community, which was pretty much one and the same. Fort Monmouth was very different, because it was our community for such a limited time. I couldn't define, even just for myself, why exactly we were going through the motions of the christening there. And yet, I wouldn't have skipped it.

Once again, the crucible of Fort Monmouth itself provided me with an answer. I barely registered the pieces of the service that came before the Sacrament of Baptism. When Reverend Robison announced us, my hold around Margaret tightened reflexively. She opened one eye and squawked in discomfort. Quiet, understanding laughter rippled through the sea of bodies in the congregation. It washed over me, too, dissolving some of my tension. Sam and I stood, turned toward those friendly faces, and I realized that, yes, not only did I belong to that place, but so did Margaret. Whether for a short time or forever, it was our community, we were connected, and it felt right to offer our daughter into the love and caring so evident right there in front of us.

Fourteen

Sam was set to be officially discharged at the end of 1945, and then we would go through another set of changes. He had been offered a job with RCA, the Radio Corporation of America, to start at the beginning of the following year. It was a solid position writing technical manuals about radios – building them, using them, and repairing them. Sam had enjoyed the challenges of military life and his position at Fort Monmouth, and he could have remained as a career officer, but he decided, and I agreed with him, that he was more suited to a position with less direct, constant interaction. He would be ready and satisfied to transfer his military involvement to the Reserve Corps and become a civilian again.

Once Sam was discharged, the Army apartment sheltering our new little family would be needed for another officer and his family. Sam had decided to build us our own house, and in the months after Margaret was born, the house materialized, brick by brick. After living all our lives with so many farms and so much open land around us, we both felt the pull of an owned piece of ground. We wanted something solid that belonged fully to us, something that would belong to those who came after us, since, amazingly, there would be at least one.

Our little house on Crest Avenue in Haddon Heights was the opposite of the old and creaky houses of our rural childhoods. It was sturdy and compact, symmetrical, centered on a neat quarter acre of suburbia. Sam built it from a Better Homes & Gardens blueprint published by Sears Roebuck. Sears sold it all then, from sewing needles to houses, and everything in between. Our house was flanked on both sides by similar sturdy, compact houses. The main part was brick, with a small, attached garage sided in white clapboard. The shutters and front door were black. The broad living room opened off the front entry to the right, and the dining room was on the left. Our small kitchen was in the back, efficient and bright with wide windows overlooking the whole backyard. The stairs and upper hallway floors were covered with a rich, swirling red and blue carpet. I took special pleasure in this choice because I'd never lived in a house with attached carpeting. The three bedrooms were spaced evenly along a central hallway, and they each had wide dormer windows. The bathroom had a modern flair, tiled in pink and black with a tub long enough to fit even Sam's great length.

Sam did all the building and finishing work by himself or with the help of a couple of other men from the base. All except for the plumbing, which he wouldn't touch. I was with Sam the first day the plumber came to meet with him at the house. The man asked me without pause if Margaret was our granddaughter. I recovered myself as quickly as I could and tried to not look too shocked. I felt so much like a young woman at the beginning of life, and I easily forgot that so many women my age were completely through motherhood, were grandmothers. In other moments, this man's question

might have unbalanced me, but that day it amused me.
No, I had a long way to go before it was my turn to be a
grandmother.

From the moment he had the plans in hand, Sam worked
diligently and doggedly to make the house real, almost
always with a smile on his face. His good cheer faded
only once, when he learned that his mother was dead.
She had tripped and fallen all the way down her long
front staircase and broken her neck.

Sam was more stunned than sad. I think it must
have seemed impossible to him that this granite woman
had any weakness, could succumb to any human fate. I
couldn't really imagine it either, so instead I envisioned a
blank space, felt a silence, where Willetta's presence had
been. That was all.

Sam had loved his mother, but I knew much of his
studied quietness came from being raised by such a sharp
and sour woman. With Willetta for a mother, it was
usually better to say nothing at all than to say the wrong
thing. I was glad that in the space of our marriage, Sam
felt free to say whatever he thought. He knew I would
love him for it, or in spite of it, either way.

Sam had never once asked his mother for money,
not once, and she had never offered any. We did just fine
on our own. When Willetta died, though, all the Purcell
money became his, and that big house, too. There were
several calls back and forth to Pennsylvania the day she
died. First the doctor called Sam with the news, then Sam
called the minister, then I called my mother and Carrol,
then Sam called Wallace Good. Without hesitation, Sam
offered the big house to the Goods, who had always been

so gracious to me, and to everyone in town, really. We had no use for that house. Neither one of us suggested the idea of taking our little family back to Pennsylvania to live. The Goods still lived in the apartment over their store, but by then so did their daughter, Idelle, along with her husband and their four children. It was manageable, but probably not too comfortable, elbows to kneecaps most of the time.

After Sam hung up the phone with Wallace Good, he sat quietly, motionless, for quite a few minutes. A weight had been lifted, but I could tell something more was on his mind, so I waited. Then Sam asked me if maybe I didn't want him to build a bigger house for us with the money we'd just inherited. I smiled at his raised eyebrows, his questioning look. Did *he* want something grander, having grown up that way? Was he afraid I would say no? Or was he more afraid I would say yes? Was he worried I would show some other, truer colors? I didn't want anything more. The new life we had was already more than I ever could have expected.

"No, of course not," I said. "The new house as it is will be just right for the three of us. I'm not a grand woman, Sam. You know that. I don't want my world getting any bigger than what I've imagined it will be, what we've imagined together."

If I'd said I'd wanted a bigger and better house, I think I would have gotten it. But at my answer, Sam's eyebrows relaxed. His face settled back into the more assured Sam I'd come to know.

Willetta had wanted to be cremated, and there would be no service for her, according to her request. I was happy Margaret was too young for all three of us to make the long trip back together easily. Sam returned to

Osceola Mills by himself to oversee the cremation, to sign over the deed to the big house to Wallace Good, and to retrieve Willetta's ashes. We never did decide on an appropriate place for them to be scattered. They remained in an urn on a shelf in the back of our tiny coat closet until we moved from Fort Monmouth to Haddon Heights. In our new house, we transferred the urn to the back corner of the bigger coat closet there. I couldn't have faced looking at a container of Willetta's ashes standing in judgement somewhere every day of my life. She hadn't been very present in our lives while she lived hers, so I didn't see why she should preside over any part of our life together now that she was dead. In Sam's defense, the placement of Willetta's ashes wasn't neglect, but simply duty at a comfortable remove. It's not always true, what they say about a man treating his wife the way he treats his mother. Not in Sam's case.

Fifteen

We moved to Crest Avenue in January 1946. Haddon Heights was only about seventy miles from Fort Monmouth, but our lives there were entirely different. Sam went to work every day at RCA and wrote about radios. I kept house and learned to be a mother.

When I think back on our first months in that house, the warmth and light of that time rises through me like bread in the oven. It wasn't warm and light outside, that's for sure. That winter of 1946 was a bitter one of perpetual snow and frigid temperatures, but the weather made me feel even more secure in the cocoon of my new inside world. As the winds blasted around the house, and the thermometer dove, I tidied my little kitchen, rocked my baby, folded clean towels straight from our new gas dryer. My content heart made me immune to the cold.

Everything about that house and our life there was small in the best way, manageable. Life felt safe and steady, neatly and completely contained. It felt so different from the vast, sprawling spaces of my earlier life, and the vast, unchallenged emptiness that had taken over my younger heart there.

In the spring, Sam planted me a garden just steps from the back kitchen door. It was only a little garden with a couple of tomato plants, a zucchini that took over everything, a cucumber plant, squash to last into the next winter, and zinnias bordering all the edges because I have always loved zinnias best. Looking out the kitchen window, squinting one eye, it seemed like I could hold the whole of the little plot in the joined palms of my upturned hands.

Our neighbors next door, Carlotta and Sal Serchia, had a garden too, but much larger. They were Italian, from South Philadelphia. Their garden seemed to tumble and sprawl all over itself, filled with tomatoes and zucchini, onions, peppers, eggplants, herbs, and melons, along with a lot of things I couldn't name. Sometimes when I surveyed it from the safety of my own yard, it seemed like the vines and leaves would be able to reach over and pull me under if I got too close. I was a more hesitant grower, wanting to nurture but afraid to hope for too much. I was glad to have only my small gathering of sturdy plants.

Carlotta rambled through her garden rows each morning, weeding, straightening, watering, picking what she needed for whatever divine thing she was cooking that day. Her side kitchen window faced onto the border of our two yards, and wonderful smells wafted through them most afternoons. Whenever I saw her in the garden and commented, she would tell me the name of the recipe she was planning. Her Italian menus were made up of things I could barely pronounce, let alone put together in my own kitchen. In Osceola we'd eaten plain, steadying food, a rotation of meat with whatever vegetables we picked or had put up in the cellar, lots of potatoes and bread, and always gravy. Our tastes had no higher expectations. Our bellies were filled most of the time, but ours was not joyous, jump-in-the-mouth food. In comparison, I thought Carlotta's meals were probably more like art.

Carlotta was tiny and wiry. She had very long hair, blacker and curlier than I'd ever seen, which she braided and wound around the top of her head. Her bun was so big and heavy, it seemed like it might topple right off her head by itself. She always wore a sackcloth apron over her dress when she picked vegetables. It was stained heavily red with sauce, and it reminded me of a butcher's apron. Carlotta was about my age, but very different. We were both quiet women, but it wasn't the same kind of quiet. She seemed self-contained, serene, easy within herself and her world. I felt like my insides swung wildly from deep worry and wariness to occasional, extreme joy. Carlotta's eyes invited you in. I don't think mine did that.

Carlotta whistled and hummed an endless, rambling tune whenever she gardened and cooked. I could hear her as I tracked behind Margaret, who by late summer of that first year was picking her way through the grass and sometimes even trying to walk. She was close enough to the ground to notice and investigate every bud and bug, and her fascination fascinated me. Still so small, my daughter was already moving ahead and away from me, while I followed close behind, always ready to catch her.

One afternoon, as the September sun thrummed heavily on every part of the house and yard, I went outside to pick a few tomatoes for our dinner. When I stepped down from the back stoop, I saw Carlotta kneeling in her garden, weeding and whistling away. I watched her for a moment, wondering again how she was so comfortable within all that riot and wildness. Then I called over to her.

"Hello? Carlotta."

She looked up, smiled at me, and returned to earth from whatever otherworldly place she'd been in.

"Hello, Louella."

Her slightly accented voice made my name into music. She was such a tiny fragment of a woman that when she stood she barely seemed to rise at all. She looked almost the same height as her tallest tomato plants. She stepped gingerly out of the vines, peeling off her yellow gardening gloves. As she walked toward me, I saw little beads of sweat on her upper lip.

"It's really a hot one, today, isn't it?" I said.

"I don't mind it so much. The air in the summer moves here more than in the city. But, yes, it is hot. Do you want to come in with me and have a limonada?"

"Ah ...?"

"Lemonade. A lemonade, I mean," she said with another smile.

I smiled back, and then I glanced hesitantly toward my own house, where Margaret was asleep. But Carlotta had never invited me in before, despite her general friendliness. There weren't too many steps between my back door and Carlotta's kitchen.

"Yes, okay. Thank you," I said.

And that was how I found myself in Carlotta's kitchen for the first time. It seemed about the same size and shape as my own. The houses were built from similar plans, I guessed, but how different her kitchen was, in so many ways that counted. A beam ran along the entire length of the ceiling above her sink and long counter. Ropes of garlic, strings of peppers, and all kinds of drying herbs were tied along it with brown kitchen twine. My kitchen tended toward light green and white, muted and functional. Carlotta's kitchen was alive with brightness. The dishes stacked on her open shelves were intense shades of red and blue and yellow. They were heavy looking, made for serious eating. Then, surprisingly, the glasses she filled with cold lemonade were identical to the daisy patterned jelly glasses lined up in my own cupboards next door.

"You really love your garden, don't you?" I said.

"Yes," she said, and she smiled with white, even teeth. "Yes, I love the garden."

"You and Sal don't have any children."

It was a statement, not a question. I was generally more considerate than that, but I'd said this before I could stop myself. Most of the other families on our new street had children, and I'd been wondering why there were none here. That day the thought just spoke itself. Maybe it was the heat, or maybe the daisy glasses.

"We had two sons. They both fought, and neither of them came home," Carlotta replied straightforwardly.

My own son would have been twenty-four by that time. Holland's age was a marker advancing itself in the recesses of my memory without effort, though in my heart I felt the loss of the infant he had been, not the boy or man he might have become. In my heart, he was still the baby I had let go, the baby I had let die. But had he lived, Holland would have been old enough to fight just like Carlotta's sons. My timeline had failed again, making me forget that a woman my age would more likely have grownup children somewhere, not young ones at home.

"I am so sorry. I really don't know why I said that to you. I'm not usually so thoughtless."

Carlotta studied me intently for a moment with a forgiving look. Her eyes probed mine.

"But you have suffered a deep sadness also, I think," she said finally. This was not a question either.

Loss has a way of tracking toward loss, like beads of water pulling together until they pool. Some people pull hard away from this force. Carlotta did not pull back. Instead, she tried to connect to everything I'd worked so hard to contain, and something inside me wouldn't let me pull away this time either.

As we sat in her kitchen with our glasses full of warming lemonade, I told Carlotta my story, much like I had told it to Sam that dark night above the orchard. Sam had listened well to me, but I knew Carlotta could absorb my words in a different, deeper way. Then Carlotta told me about how she had encouraged her sons to enlist, to be proud of their adopted country, to be ready to contribute. She described how she'd gloated just a bit that her sons were on the side of rightness, fighting for America and not for Italy. Then they both died, unprotected by their Americanness.

Two mothers together, we spoke of ushering new life into the world only to suffer its loss. We spoke of guilt, of endurance. We spoke of the emptiness that can be covered over, but never truly filled up.

The Serchias had dozens of Italian relatives who still lived in South Philadelphia, and it was not surprising for many of them to show up in the backyard next door on any warm, clear Saturday night. While Margaret was growing up, Sam and I didn't socialize all that much, satisfied by the simple company of our small family. But when the Serchias had a party, we went.

Carlotta was always ready and waiting with food, and Sal with wine and music to go with it. Sal played the violin, and if he wasn't pouring wine, he was playing, casually strolling around his small kingdom. The children usually spilled over into our backyard on those party nights, and Margaret ran right along with the pack. She was generally as reserved as Sam and I were in large groups, but not in that large group. On these warm nights the Purcell reserve loosened as we were caught up in the intensity of those happy Italians.

Sometimes I joined Carlotta in the kitchen, talking with her while she cooked. I don't know how Carlotta managed to produce so much food in her small kitchen, the same size as mine, but she fed these masses wreathed in smiles. She was so efficient without ever seeming harried. She didn't like me to get in the way by trying to help, but she liked to have company. She drank wine while she cooked, and I drank wine in her kitchen, too, which was something I rarely did anywhere else. When it got too hot inside, I would pick up the plates of whatever was ready and step out into the yard. Colorful, hot-blooded life swirled and ran at my feet, and in that time and place it didn't feel overwhelming. It felt good and right, and I felt easy within those moments.

Through so many years together on Crest Avenue, I would think back again and again to my first visit in Carlotta's kitchen, the first of many such hours. I was forever grateful for the kindness in Carlotta's eyes that afternoon. It had invited me in, invited me to stay.

Sixteen

Within our sum of days, there are a few that remain whole, preserved and protected. The details are alive and touchable still, layered inside you – what you wore, what you smelled, what you said, and most of all, how you felt.

Margaret's first day of school is like that. I still have every detail of that morning. As I braided segments of her brown hair carefully back and forth, little bits of curl wrapped around my fingers. How had we arrived here so fast? In an hour, I would be walking her to the elementary school. First grade. She was tidy and ready in her red checkered dress, white bobby socks, and shiny new saddle shoes. She just needed the red ribbon I was about to tie onto the end of her finished braid.

She was wide-eyed, chatty, excited to get to work, meet the challenge, barrel toward whatever was up next. This was how Margaret approached most of life. She'd been waiting and wanting to go to school for what seemed like every day of her six years, watching the kids up and down Crest Avenue set off on foot and on bikes each school morning. Today it was finally her turn. Her impatience filled our small, still house.

I was as ready as I could be, too, ready for her to explore and learn more than I could teach her. But her constant companionship had filled my days, so school would be a big shift for both of us.

It was my habit to think ahead through challenges, to reach out and feel my way towards the possible outcomes, to work through any obstacles and upsets that might otherwise take me by surprise. That first school morning, my usual approach left me feeling too lonely, as if I'd be walking home missing an arm or a leg, or worse, leaving some of my insides behind. I didn't want a shred of my worry or self-pity to change Margaret's enthusiasm and curiosity. Instead, I focused all my attention on tying a red ribbon on the end of a brown braid, making the bow symmetrical, tight and secure.

Many school days came and went after that, and I adjusted to the rhythm of the school year as smoothly as I could. Margaret excelled, intent on learning anything and everything in the classroom and in the world. Most of her first-grade year, I walked her back and forth to school. On our walks home, she told me all about the happenings of the school day and what she thought about it all. Even then, Margaret had a precise knack for cutting right through words and actions straight to motivation. She was not unkind, but she was very honest and not always empathetic. I often wondered when she would turn the revealing beam of her analysis on me.

Most mornings after I walked Margaret to school, I walked myself down to Swicker's Corner Store to get the newspaper for Sam to read when he got home from work. Sometimes I got milk or eggs or whatever else I might need in between our weekly trips to the real grocery store. We could've had the paper delivered, or Sam could have stopped on his way home, but the walk had become part of my routine, adding structure to my first hour while Margaret was at school.

Each day when I walked out of Swicker's, I faced the Catholic church, St. Augustine, which stood on the corner across from the store. It didn't look black and brooding like the Catholic church in Osceola Mills always had to me. It was dark, but it beckoned. It intrigued me with a sense of sad and benevolent mystery. St. Augustine was Carlotta's church. It seemed to invite me in, much like her eyes.

Since we'd moved into our house, I hadn't been to any church regularly. Haddon Heights was big enough that there were two Methodist churches to choose from. Sam and I had been to services at both. We'd also tried the First Presbyterian Church, and then the Episcopal Church, St. Stephen's. Then we'd stopped trying, because not one of those places felt right to me. Instead they'd each felt hollow, and I knew by then that church wasn't meant to feel that way. In each of those churches, I'd tried to reach down inside myself, to take hold of and pull up the feeling I'd known briefly at Fort Monmouth. That Christmas warmth and solidarity, the sense of belonging I'd had at Margaret's baptism. Those were the feelings I was grasping for. I tried to overlay those ideas of community and communion on these new places, but I was unsuccessful. It just wouldn't stick. Sam had found his church in his work. He found that feeling of connection and higher power in the concrete and theoretical magic of science, of putting inanimate bits and pieces together and making them into something alive. But I was still seeking.

It took a long time, almost a year of walking to Swicker's every day, before I finally crossed the street and went into St. Augustine. As I passed through the dark doorway, I felt a longed-for peace wash over me. This felt like church the way it should feel, the way it was supposed to make me feel, like my soul was escaping the bounds of my body. There I stood at ten o'clock on a Tuesday morning, newspaper in one hand and carton of cream in the other, as a part of me separated, lifted away, and danced in the vaults of that high-ceilinged old building.

From that day on, almost every morning after Margaret was at school, I stopped in at St. Augustine. It didn't feel right to dip my fingers in the holy water font or to cross myself. These rituals didn't have real meaning for me. But at the back of the sacristy, I would light two memorial candles and quiet my thoughts. Then I would sit in the very last pew. I didn't close my eyes to pray. Instead I looked up, watching the sunlight stream through the rich rainbow of the stained-glass windows. In the dust motes and morning quiet of that Catholic sanctuary, I had finally found a place for myself.

Seventeen

After we'd moved to New Jersey, we didn't travel back to Pennsylvania often, but when my mother died, of course there was no question of going or not. She'd had a heart condition for several years before she died. Carrol had told me she was declining, her body growing weaker and frail, even though she had still sounded mostly like herself when we talked on the phone each week.

She died in 1957, deep into July. *Hot as Hades* she would have said if she'd still been there to comment. Lenore, Angelica, John, Austin, Carrol, and I, along with all the husbands, wives, and children, and what seemed like the entire town of Osceola Mills, were packed into the Methodist church for the funeral service. We were a mass of dark figures almost paralyzed by the heat. My mother had been well liked for her no-nonsense approach to rural life and death. Her life had not been easy, and I think many of our neighbors had taken strength from her example over so many years. I wasn't like her in this way. If I'd inherited any of the fibrous, resilient stuff she was made of, it was scant among my many other, more delicate strands.

Until my mother died, Angelica and I had not seen each other since Sam and I had gotten married, when she had attended our wedding and I'd done my best to ignore that she was there. She'd been right when she'd said there would be no baby of her own, and I saw the pain of this barrenness plain on her face each time she looked at Margaret during that visit. If I'd liked Angelica more from the beginning, at the root, maybe she and I could have been some comfort to each other when little Holland had died, and through any other hardships our lives handed over. But not liking her had made it so much easier to cut her off. Comfort and compassion between us were made impossible by blame and anger. I assigned blame to myself for giving the baby away to Angelica, but I'd pinned as much of my anger as I could to her.

That day of our mother's funeral, as we stood at the gravesite, my anger and sorrow and blame were all stowed deep inside me, held tightly in check by my cloak of marriage and motherhood. As dust joined dust, I breathed in the hot, green air. I looked intently down at my hand joined with Margaret's. I studied the shape of our black shoes, solid and dark against the summer grass as Sam stood tall behind us, wrapping us completely in his long shadow.

Eighteen

As all our days were dealt out into the ebb and flow of years, and Margaret grew up, I never considered telling her about the baby I'd had and then lost. Not once. That's not to say I didn't think about it, the fact that she didn't know anything about him. But I never thought there was a reason she should know.

She did know that I'd been married to someone else before I was married to Sam. I don't really remember how or when she came to know this part of the story. It wasn't something I'd told her deliberately, but I didn't keep it from her either. Even though we didn't visit my family in Pennsylvania often, we were there enough times that Holland's name and the fact of my earlier marriage must have come out in reference to something or in some part of conversation. By the time Margaret and I talked about it, she was nine or ten, and the question came out more as a statement, like we were picking up the end of previous discussion.

"*How* old were you when you got married the first time?" she had asked, as if for verification.

"Nineteen," was my reply. I had to hold myself back from saying anything else or asking any question in return until I could know what more she might ask or say.

"And then you married Dad when you were *forty?*"
At that she raised her eyebrows in the way that made her
look just like Sam.

"Yes."

"Wow." She had nodded in closure. The
conversation had begun and ended with no more to it
than that.

My earlier marriage was not a thing that shaped
Margaret's sense of who I was to her or who she was as my
child. Even when she grew up and was ready to get
married herself, even then she asked me nothing more
about my first marriage, only saying that she hoped her
married life would be as close and content as the life Sam
and I had together.

When she said that, I'm not sure what my face
revealed. I had a hard time thinking of Margaret as ever
being content. To me, that word meant an easiness of
spirit. Though my daughter and I were very different in
temperament, neither one of us had an easy spirit.
Margaret raced headlong at each part of her life,
challenging herself, challenging the world. She always
seemed to want everyone around her to do better, to live
up to her standards, her sense of responsibility and
forthrightness. It's difficult for that approach to meet
with ease for too very long. But if *content* wears its
simplest definition, *to be satisfied*, then I imagine each of
us can find her own path to it, in her own way, in her
own time.

Separate from my earlier marriage, the baby Holland
and the loss of him were topics no one in my family ever
talked about. It was like all trace of him had been buried
with his tiny body. To talk about him would have been to

dig up loss, guilt, shame, bitterness, and sisterly contempt. It would have done no one any good, and they knew it.

Carlotta tried to talk about him, to get me to talk about him. She was the only one. She called my attention to the bitterness I still carried in my heart and how it could spread its spoilage into other parts of me. She urged me to talk about the baby, to talk about Angelica, to talk about how the shadows of my earlier life shaped how I was with my daughter. I knew Carlotta's insistence came from a place of sincerity and love. She knew loss as I did, but her loss had not created in her the same black hole that mine had opened in me.

Even as she lay close to the end of her own life, in some of our last conversations, Carlotta still tried. In those moments, I think she wanted to include me in what she was experiencing, the complete stripping away and letting go of life's sadness and regret in the soul's pursuit of peace. But I selfishly hardened my defenses, even as I wept with her, for her.

Why do we say *all of a sudden* to define changes that occur over weeks or months or years, changes that shouldn't take us by surprise? Because sometimes the realization of that vast difference between what *was* and what *is* does feel sudden. It felt like this to me when Margaret got married and was really gone, even though I'd been there for each and every day up until then. And when Margaret told me she and her husband, John, were trying to have a baby, my resolve wavered for the first time. Would it be right to tell her about my first baby, who had not been her?

Margaret had finished college with honors, gone after and gotten a reporting job, met the right man, gotten married. True to form, she'd laid out a plan and followed it. She'd checked off all the boxes, done what she'd set out to do and done it well. Then she was ready to take a break and have a baby, but her body wasn't. For what seemed like the first time, Margaret was not in control of how and when she accomplished something. I think she felt cheated, defeated, felt the loss of something before she ever really had it. The strength of her will and all her wanting were not enough.

As Margaret went through this heartache, I felt more needed by my adult daughter than I ever had when she was small, but I couldn't revel in that need. Each time we talked on the phone, her tears came with such forcefulness from the deep. I had to reach back through the years to recognize her, because this was not the adult Margaret I had grown used to. In her anguish, I heard the child she had been, frustrated with herself at not being able to ride her new two-wheeler on the first try, angry about not getting a tap dance move just so, worried about scoring a perfect mark on the last chemistry test of the semester. She yoked this failure heavily to herself, carrying the weight of it with her usual determination. I knew that particular kind of self-punishment. I knew it all too well. I wanted to lift this misery from her, my little girl, to tell her all I knew about harrowing heartbreak and lack of control.

Maybe telling her about the baby who would have been her brother would have helped her. Maybe it would have made me more real to her. But it might have made it even worse, that I'd managed to have two babies after all, while she seemed unable to have one. I wouldn't take that risk. I worried that Margaret might think I was forcing sympathy in my own direction. I also worried that adding my own story to hers would just add to the tide of sadness rising inside her, and I couldn't do that. She was still my baby, after all, the one I had gotten to keep.

Nineteen

Margaret may never know how deep and wide my happiness was when she finally had a baby, when my daughter became a mother. I was taken by surprise myself by the engulfing feeling of completeness I felt at Sarah's arrival. When I became a grandmother, I became yet another version of myself.

Margaret, John, and Sarah live in a big neighborhood house in northern New Jersey, about two hours away from us in Haddon Heights. Sam and I have visited them there only a handful of times. As we get older, the drive seems longer. Plus, I don't think we fit too well into the rhythm of Margaret's brisk, suburban household. It's easier for her to slow her pace a little when she comes back to our house, when she's back in our known world, than for us to try to keep up with hers.

Sarah comes often to stay overnight with us on her own. We meet about halfway to do a hand off, at a sprawling rest stop off the Blackhorse Pike. Sam and I always get there first. We're parked and waiting when Margaret's wood-paneled station wagon pulls into the parking lot. Sarah barely waits until Margaret has stopped the car all the way before she unbuckles herself from the middle of the backseat. She's over to us so quickly that I need to wait to open my own car door until she comes to a full stop and then backs up a step or two. Otherwise I might knock her clear over. In one hand, she always clutches a stuffed animal, a different companion for each journey. Sarah has a zoo's worth of stuffed animals. Her other hand and arm come at me for a great big squeeze, catching me around the knees and thighs. Still holding onto me, she waves to Sam with her animal-filled hand. In these joyful handover moments, there are never any tears from Sarah. She hardly even glances back at her mother.

Sometimes Margaret gets out of the car for a quick hug and then a wave to her father. Sometimes she stays in the driver's seat and just opens the window to say hello and goodbye. Then she drives away, a mix of guilt and relief pulling her smile into a grimace. On these days, Margaret has shed motherhood and transferred a precious, time-sensitive gift to me. Until we exchange back, I will stretch and knead the hours with Sarah, making them expand and rise and fill me with warmth.

When Margaret pulls away, Sarah and I get back into the car with Sam, and Sarah scrambles onto the hump in between the two front seats of our big blue Plymouth. This is her designated spot.

What would it have been like to have Margaret settle in next to me while I was at the wheel? I always wonder this as Sarah gets comfortable, arranging her animal of the day on her lap. Stubbornly, I never did get my driver's license. Right after Margaret was born, Sam tried to teach me to drive, but it didn't stick. Once we moved to Haddon Heights, I decided I could just walk anywhere I really needed to go when Sam wasn't home. Our little house, my garden, the backyard, the two willow trees at its edge, they contained all I really needed in the world then.

I felt this limitation was a good one, that it kept our life in control and closely held to home. But now I have moments of wishing I'd had some wider adventures with my daughter.

Now, when Sarah visits, sometimes she asks me why we can only go to the supermarket or to get ice cream when Grandpa is home, and I remind her that I don't have a driver's license.

"But why not?" she questions. "My mommy always drives me everywhere."

And I reply that I always like to have Grandpa for company. And that seems to make obvious sense to her.

Twenty

I've felt it so many times, the expanding and contracting of each day, each month, each year. They all combine and then compress into one whole life. I've stopped trying to define this ebb and flow, stopped allowing myself to be surprised by it. These days I climb the stairs more slowly than I used to, but still under my own power. These are still my feet moving me, as I put one in front of the other. This is still my hand firmly grasping the mahogany banister, worn smooth with all our years of holding on.

As I went up the stairs last night, it was to the cadence of Sarah's little voice coming through the closed door of the back bedroom. She's four now. I stood still for a moment. My whole being just wanted to listen to her, to absorb her being there. Sarah was *dreaming*. That's what she calls it, this habit of continuous, out-loud improvisation. She's her own best entertainment most of the time. This makes her an easy visitor and good company for me, a woman who's always lived a lot of life inside her own head.

When Sarah comes to stay overnight, she calls it her *Grandma time*. Sometimes I still have trouble believing I'm the grandma. My life began again when I was forty, so I always imagined old age as somewhere in the far distance. I think sometimes it can feel like we're standing still, not moving or changing at all, because even as we speed toward the horizon, everything else around us is moving, too. But then how would I have gotten here, how did I get to be seventy-five?

Listening to Sarah chattering along on the other side of the door last night sparked a happiness that lit my whole being. I didn't want to pop the moment, but it was time for dinner, and I had too many things going on the stove downstairs to hover outside the bedroom for too long. I tapped on the door with a finger, one that's a little crooked with arthritis now.

"Sarah, it's Grandma. Are you in there?"

"Grand*ma*... of course I'm in here. Where else would I be?"

Her broad grin and a raised eyebrow greeted me as she opened the door. She wasn't at all self-conscious about being caught talking away to herself. She's not the self-conscious sort. Her thick brown hair was sticking out like a mane, frizzy and kinked from the braids I'd woven into it after her bath last night. At least my hands were not too old for hair styling yet. Sarah looks more like her father than like Margaret, but her intelligence and her observance of the world are as keen as her mother's. Even at four she's in a constant state of analysis.

"Is it time to come down for dinner, Grandma?"

She knew I'd made her favorite meal. Roast beef, salty and slow-cooked until it falls apart, mashed potatoes with gravy, and peach parfait for dessert. In fact, Sarah probably thinks this is the only meal I know how to cook, since I make it whenever she comes to stay with Sam and me. I don't think this counts against me, though. My granddaughter and I love each other in that unmodified way that seems almost impossible between parent and child. At least it always seemed unreachable with Margaret. That one degree of separation has made all the difference for Sarah and me.

"Yes, it's dinnertime. You can come down and help me set the table," I told her.

I moved one at a time down the carpeted steps into the bedroom. I went over to the wide Jenny Lind bed, which had been Margaret's, to straighten the bedclothes. I plumped the pillow. I smoothed out the bunched blanket. This was the blanket I crocheted right before Margaret was born, the one I never thought was quite right for a baby. Through the years, it had made the rounds of our whole house. It matched nothing but ended up everywhere. Finally, it had come to rest on the end of Margaret's bed.

It felt like it had been only a breath since I was braiding Margaret's hair, walking her home from school, fixing her lunch. Where did all that time go?

I could see where it had gone. All those years, all those ordinary moments, were preserved within me, and the sum of them was contained in the smile of the little girl in front of me.

I took Sarah's warm little hand in mine, and we made our way together down the stairs and into the dining room. Sam was already sitting down, with his chair pulled back from the table, one long leg slung over the other. He smiled readily. Sarah walked over and patted his cheek. They're not snuggly, but Sam loves Sarah in his own quiet, uncomplicated way, and she knows it. He's a lot like he was with Margaret when she was Sarah's size.

Sometimes after dinner, Sarah climbs up onto Sam's lap and asks if she can have a spoonful of jelly from the cut glass jar I keep on the table. He always looks to me before answering, checking wordlessly for my okay. Only I know whether she's already had this treat earlier in the day. Last night, when I started to clear away the dirty dishes and saw Sarah eyeing up the jelly jar, I shook my head *no*, but when I was gone back into the kitchen and out of sight, I think Sam probably gave her a spoonful of jelly anyway.

Sarah has been here for two days this time, a longer visit than usual. This afternoon, instead of meeting in the middle, Margaret drove all the way to our house to collect Sarah. Having my daughter back in the house is always two parts joy and one part sorrow.

The first joy is my love for her, and the love I have for the woman she's become. Margaret is more confident about who she is and more certain about the world than I ever was.

The second joy, which magnifies the first, is watching Margaret with her own daughter. I wonder at the easy back and forth I witness between them. Did Margaret ever climb onto my lap like that? Did she walk into my bedroom without knocking like that? Did I ever stroke her hair or gently squeeze her hand in that way, just because she was next to me?

The sorrow wrapped around these strands of joy comes from knowing our visit is almost over. Sam and I see Margaret and Sarah often, but there will be a stretch of quiet, ordinary time in between. The days will take on their usual rhythm again, and I'll go through my routines smoothly enough, but the first hours after they leave always feel deflated, deeply stilled, like some vital piece of me has been misplaced.

Today I walked out to the driveway with Margaret and Sarah when it was time for them to get on their way. When my girls, big and small, were in the car ready to go, and I was back inside, I turned a chair away from the dining table to face the front window and sat down to watch them. I pulled the weighty blue curtain aside and waved. Margaret gave a quick wave and a half smile. Then, looking over her shoulder, she backed surely down the short driveway, over the bump, and out into the street. Sarah grinned her grin and waved furiously, continuously. When their car was pointed in the direction of home, Sarah stopped waving and pointed herself in the direction of home, too. As they drove down Crest Avenue and turned the corner, my heart swelled and constricted with those unequal measures of joy and sorrow. I had lost them again for now.

I didn't sit for long, though. This time the restored quiet of my house was less lonely. I had an idea, and I had to act on it before I changed my mind.

Sarah always asks me if I'm sure I don't have a china doll or some high button shoes I've forgotten about in the attic or basement. I don't, and she knows it. The few possessions I'd had as a child were made over and passed down until they pretty much fell apart. But Sarah still asks passionately each time she visits, and I think what she really wants is to understand a feeling she can't pin a label to. This child has nostalgia for places she's never been and people she's never met. She has a deep-down perception, even at so very young an age, of how connected she is to all of it. When Margaret was a child, her mind was always reaching up and out, but Sarah is different. Her senses stretch in every direction.

I wish I did have a pair of high button shoes or a bisque-faced doll to give her. I would hand them off with a happy heart, knowing they would mean more to Sarah than they ever had to me. Life is so full of things. They all seem so necessary at one time, but they're ultimately meaningless. Sheets and towels, shoes and measuring cups, hammers, tire gauges, spare buttons. What are we meant to do with it all?

I've gotten good at throwing off all these trappings. When I start to feel the heaviness of life pressing on and around me, both the love and the loss, I close my eyes and dismiss all these items like the shedding of a skin. I dive into a deep pool, leaving a varied trail of objects as I go farther and farther down. I dive until I am too deep to return, until I've let everything go, and my soul floats alone. I'm surprised sometimes by how strongly that piece of me longs for release. There are so many who fight so hard to hold onto it all and are forced out of life anyway, before they're ready to go. I guess a bit of this feeling has always been with me, though. It's not just a function of age.

Earlier this morning, Sarah hadn't come into my bedroom to get me as usual. The birds chirping is her signal that it's time to get up, but this morning there was no Sarah, no little bare feet murmuring toward me across the red and blue carpet. So I walked quietly down the hall myself to make sure everything was all right. When I'd pushed the door open, there she was, curled up on the bed in the rose covered blanket. She was awake, her eyes open, but they were focused on a realm beyond my seeing. After a few seconds, she sat up, reorienting.

"Hi Grandma," she'd said.

As Sarah pulled the blanket onto her lap, I was struck. However gaudy and misfit it was, maybe this was the relic she needed. The blanket wasn't high button shoes or a china doll, but it would do. I decided then that I'd give it to her, and I would give her a story to go with it. I was sure she would keep it well.

Twenty-one

Now, my story is told. It's written down and made real again. Too thick to go into an envelope, I've folded and tied the papers together with a bit of cotton hem facing I dug out of my odds and ends drawer.

I sat at the dining table through the whole afternoon, my grocery tablet in front of me. I thought and wrote, reliving moments in a life that seems totally foreign and unconnected to who I am now at seventy-five. Sam sat in the living room, right through the time he would usually come into the kitchen to make us some coffee. Somehow, he knew I needed to be by myself even as I sat there plainly in the dining room. Sam and I have been married a long time now, and he has loved me well for all of it.

Dear Sarah, is how I started, just like any other, everyday letter. But this letter is a pouring out of so much more, an unburdening long overdue. Writing this letter to Sarah has wrung more out of me than I knew was left. Most of the people who knew this story of my first life, who knew of the baby Holland at all, are already dead, and I could have left the story untold, but that didn't seem right. Something inside me knows that the telling of it, even if only in a letter for now, will bind together the separate pieces of my soul long after my body has let go and I'm gone.

I tuck the letter into the folds of the blanket. I wrap the blanket in tissue paper and then again in a brown paper grocery sack. I take the package upstairs and place it gently on the top shelf of the cedar closet. Margaret still uses this closet when she visits. She hangs her nightgown and robe on the inside hook, then stows her bags and things on the closet floor. She's never tolerated clutter. She needs her space to be as regimented and orderly as her mind.

When Margaret sees this package sitting on the shelf with its air of waiting, she will leave it be. She'll ask me about it, and I will tell her it's for Sarah, but not just yet. And she'll be satisfied with my answer. My daughter is intelligent and seeking, but I think she's finally learning to be patient when she needs to be. I think she's gathering this patience from being a mother. I think she's beginning to understand that everything in life is not for knowing all at once.

Margaret

Twenty-two

Margaret had never really known her mother, or let her mother know her. She'd always been pushing past Louella, unable or unwilling to slow down enough to ask the right questions or listen well to any answers. Margaret needed to be different, better. And no matter what she did, what she accomplished, it never seemed to be enough or to be the right thing in Louella's eyes. Louella seemed to hold her daughter at arm's length, always assessing, and this reserve made Margaret hold herself away, too, even in moments when she didn't really want to. Maybe that was every mother, every daughter, Margaret thought later. But by then it was too late for them to let each other in.

It's early on a Tuesday morning, not even light out yet. Margaret is wide awake. Her husband, John, has been in Albany since yesterday taking a deposition. Margaret misses him, but feels the luxury of having the bed, the whole house, to herself.

It's her day off, but this morning she won't stay in bed too long. She has an agenda. She's going to sort through the cedar chest to get out some baby things for Sarah. In just three months, Sarah will become a mother herself. How much better and easier the whole process has been for Sarah, Margaret thinks. The transition from wanting a baby to having a new life, a new perfect little person, on the way has been almost seamless for her daughter.

After breakfast, Margaret goes back upstairs and into the guest room. Her old cedar chest stands at the foot of the guest bed, squat and enduring. She lifts the lid, and a wave of sharp, clean scent quickens her nostrils. It conjures the feeling of standing inside her mother's cedar closet, and it's not unpleasant. Margaret lets the lid of the chest fall back until it rests open against the foot of the brass bedstead.

The first thing she lifts out of the chest is the red tartan skirt Sarah wore to the first day of first grade. This will go to Sarah, Margaret decides, even though the baby won't be able to wear it for years. She knows Sarah will remember it. Next, Margaret takes out two baby blankets. The yellow one is soft and smooth, ready to be loved again. The pink one is edged with satin ribbon and embroidered cornflowers. It's beautiful but scratchy, and Margaret puts it aside to be returned to the chest later. After the blankets, she lifts out a little boy's wool coat, navy blue and trimmed with toggle closures. She'd unearthed this treasure at a church rummage sale, and had bought it, hoping. But she was never able to use it after all. Next, there is a heavy wool blanket, Army issue, from her father's days at Fort Monmouth. While Margaret was growing up, this blanket had lived in the trunk of successive cars, pulled out for picnics or to wrap around something as extra padding. Beneath the Army blanket, carefully packed in the palest peach tissue paper, is Margaret's wedding veil, a long single layer of delicate antique lace.

Thirty-five years ago, this veil had trailed down Margaret's back and spread out behind her, longer even than the train of her wedding dress. The moments just before the ceremony are still vivid. She'd stood in the back vestibule of the church, poised, a parent on each side, listening for the change in music. Sam was ready to take her arm, but he sensed that Louella needed a separate moment, and he stepped aside. Louella's soft hand cupped her daughter's cheek lightly, and she looked into Margaret's eyes with an uncharacteristic tenderness.

"I thought I missed you before," she said. "When you went away to school, when you were gone from home, I thought I missed you. But in this moment, I miss you the most."

Louella didn't say anything more. She did not hold Margaret close or place a kiss on her cheek. She simply pulled the front piece of lace down over Margaret's face and turned her by the shoulder toward Sam, her expression veiled from her daughter.

In the cedar chest beneath Margaret's veil is the cross-stitched ballet scene she'd made as a birthday gift for Sarah when she turned nine. Sarah had loved to dance so much when she was a little girl, and for a while everything in her room had been about ballet. In the picture Margaret had made, faceless, pink-legged figures in black leotards mark ballet positions across the fabric, each one distinguishable only by height and hair color. Margaret's needlepoint skills had always been basic at best, and she'd followed a pattern precisely to make this gift. Sarah had always remarked how funny it was that each figure seemed to match a different girl in her own ballet class.

Now Margaret has reached the bottom of the chest, and she finds what she's really been looking for. She lifts out a package wrapped in brown paper and tied with a long bit of brown hem facing. This package is heavy for its size, and it's been waiting a long time to be retrieved.

Twenty-three

For ten years after Sam died, Louella lived alone and untethered in their house on Crest Avenue, two hours away from where Margaret lived. She made it there on her own until she was ninety.

Sam had suffered through years and years of Parkinson's disease. Bit by bit it had stolen his mobility, his ability to feed himself, his speech, and then, swiftly, everything else. Time and time again as Sam's condition declined, Margaret had tried to talk to her mother about their options. Sam couldn't drive anymore, and her mother had never had a license, so they were completely housebound. Louella was a strong woman, but she was not young, and Sam was a giant of a man. Maneuvering him around the house taxed her body, though Margaret thought maybe it taxed her heart even more.

Louella finally agreed to have an elevator chair installed when Sam couldn't climb the stairs anymore. It was important to her that he could still sleep in his own bed each night. But that was it. She did everything else for him by herself, and with an almost combative approach. Margaret finally gave up, gave in to this stubbornness. She stopped trying to convince her mother to move Sam to some type of facility or to have someone into the house to help care for him. Louella wanted no help, no charity, no sympathy, not even from her daughter. Especially not from Margaret.

Margaret didn't take Sarah to visit Louella and Sam much while Sam was sick, something she later regretted. It should have been just the opposite, but that house was not a pleasant place for a little girl. Louella did make it to the bitter end, all by herself. She and Sam were together, independent, until the moment Sam died. When Margaret arrived the next day, she felt broken in half with misunderstanding. She hoped that when she was old herself, maybe she would understand better. Or even if she didn't, she would at least not push against the people who loved her to gain the strength she needed. She decided that when she was old, if Sarah offered help, she would lean on her daughter and love her even more for it.

Sal Serchia still lived next door, and after Sam died, Sal checked on Louella every day, even if just to wave between her back stoop and his kitchen window. When he didn't see her one morning, he walked over and knocked on her back door, and then at the front door, on and off for fifteen minutes. When Louella still didn't answer, Sal called Margaret, and then called the local police. They got the door down and found Louella lying on her bedroom floor, dehydrated and disoriented. That was the day Margaret was forced to admit the situation had to change.

Margaret found a room available in a nursing home close to her own house. Every atom of her being protested this step, fought against the defeat of moving her mother to a place that was called a home but wasn't really. But

Louella refused to come and live with her daughter, even though Sarah was grown up, and there was more than enough room.

Margaret and Louella worked together to clean out and pack up the little house that had been Louella's home for almost fifty years, and this sorting was much more efficient than Margaret had expected it to be. The material things that populate a life, even such a whittled down life, are many and varied, but Louella must have begun the whole process much, much earlier, at least in the rooms of her own mind. In those rooms, all was curated and culled. Louella had already decided what to keep and what to pitch. She was the last to go.

Now, on this morning so many years past that wrenching transition, Margaret sits very still on the side of the guest room bed, holding the brown paper package she's unearthed from the cedar chest. In the quiet she can almost put herself back into that last day in the house of her childhood.

They'd turned off the inside lights, but late afternoon sunlight spilled in through the dormer windows in her old bedroom. Louella asked Margaret to reach this package, high up on a shelf, the last thing left in the cedar closet. Margaret had seen it there countless times, and she knew it held the garish white blanket covered in bright, reckless roses that she'd made before Margaret was born.

The blanket had migrated around their house until Margaret claimed it because her bedroom was always the coldest. One day when Margaret was visiting with Sarah, Louella had shown her the package wrapped up in the closet and told her she had put the blanket away for Sarah, for when Sarah became a mother. She did not elaborate. Sarah was only four then, and Margaret wondered why Louella thought Sarah would ever want the blanket, and what explanation she, Margaret, would be able to offer to her daughter, since by that time Louella herself would most likely be gone.

On that final day, packing up everything in her mother's house, when Louella had asked Margaret to get the package down for her, she took it from her daughter's hands, closed her eyes, and clasped it to her heart with a kind of reverence Margaret had never witnessed up close before.

Margaret puts the package down next to her on the bed and unties the hem facing still holding it closed. She unfolds the brown paper, and then a layer of white tissue paper. She studies the contents in the truth-telling morning sunlight. The blanket is just the same as she remembers it. Margaret is not sure Sarah will even remember it. But even if she doesn't, Margaret knows Sarah will cry. She will cry, even if afterward she just folds the blanket up and tucks it away again in a closet somewhere.

Margaret pulls the blanket out of its paper. The thick wool is heavy with years of waiting. As she unfolds the top corner, ready to spread the blanket out in front of her, she sees a bundle of folded papers, tied with the same brown hem facing. Her insides give a little start. *Sarah* is written on the outside paper in the loopy scrawl of Louella's old age. Margaret feels unaccustomed tears quicken at the corners of her eyes as she confronts this present day offering from a mother whose mind and body are long removed.

Twenty-four

Sarah visited Margaret's parents often for overnights when she was small, before she started school. Margaret would meet Louella and Sam at a rest stop halfway between her house and theirs. On the way, Margaret would always feel a creep of guilt about how sharply she was anticipating her day of freedom. At the same time, she was always disappointed that Sarah didn't seem to miss her an ounce.

Sarah would fly out of their car and hurtle her little body at Louella without a backward glance or single tear. Margaret always watched with joyful guilt, vexed that she could be so hurt by Sarah's lack of attachment to her while at the same time Margaret couldn't wait to drive away with only herself.

Sometimes Margaret thought having only one child took a lot more energy than having more than one. She only had one shot, one opportunity to do motherhood right. Margaret was used to doing everything right.

She'd gone to college to be a journalist because she was a good researcher, a capable writer. She liked things defined and structured. She liked order. She liked the facts. After graduation, she got a good job at a small regional newspaper in Trenton. Margaret was the only woman on the news floor, and she was mostly proofreading and fact checking, but she liked the work and the pace of the newsroom. It was black and white and brisk. John was the roommate of her college roommate's husband, in his last year of law school when they met. They got married, bought a house, and set up their happy lives together.

Margaret knew that someday she would want a family. Isn't that what every woman wanted? A family? But when that day came, when she was finally ready, just wanting a baby wasn't enough to make it happen. And then there was only one. Their family was a familiar triangle shape.

When Margaret held Sarah for the first time, in that very first moment she knew she didn't want to be in the newsroom anymore. She couldn't imagine wanting to be anywhere besides where her baby was for a long, long time. And for someone like Margaret, who thrived on facts, order, momentum, and structure, this undeniable reaction was unexpected and unsettling.

As the first bloom of euphoria and attachment that accompanied Sarah's arrival receded, Margaret felt lost and blundering in a thicket of exhaustion and inexperience most of the time. Since she'd chosen not to go back to work, Sarah became her work. And what explanation would Margaret be able to offer herself or the rest of the world about the job she was doing, about the kind of mother she was, if Sarah were less than exceptional?

When Margaret felt like she needed a break, some space to breathe and think, her own restlessness infuriated her. It had taken her so long to become someone's mother once she'd decided to do it. And even in the clearing breaths, when Margaret was apart from

Sarah, there was a poised waiting presence, the specter of imminent reentry, and guilt right alongside it, and so Margaret felt like she was never truly alone.

If Margaret could have found her breath and slowed down without removing herself, she would have realized that motherhood was less like trying to find your way out of a thicket, less a journey, and more a cycle, more like throwing a pot. She'd learned this process once upon a time in college when she'd had to choose a creative elective. With the wheel spinning in front of you, the damp clay like cool, smooth velvet under your fingertips, you focus intently, always keeping constant contact. You shape and mold, guiding by feel with gentle, constant force. You hold the center, trying to recognize symmetry in its perfect roundness the instant it's reached. Round and round and round. But a lot like clay, children are unpredictable. They're made of a changeable substance, and there are many rogue forces at work. And, as the experienced potter will tell you, the finishing process can be infinite.

Now that Sarah is grown up and gone, Margaret misses her. Always. Oh, to be lost and blundering with her again, even just for a few hours, a day, Margaret thinks. She hopes that when Sarah is the mother of a daughter herself, she will be able to find a middle space between the clearing and the thicket, a place to take a breath without exiting, a place where the path is narrow and often uphill, but the way is true and clear. It's a place Margaret could never find for herself, but she is sure her daughter will be a quicker study.

Twenty-five

When Margaret was growing up, it was not usual for her mother to show a lot of emotion. Any sadness, anger, even joy, seemed to have to fight its way out of some constantly patrolled inner space. Louella didn't talk about her past very often. She lived each day as it happened. She didn't choose to draw many connections for Margaret between the child she had been and the child Margaret was. Louella was domestic and practical, as most mothers were then. She was not coddling, not overly harsh either. Sometimes, though, her demeanor was punctuated by inexplicable moments of fierceness, big feelings escaping despite her best efforts to contain them. Since these times were few and far between, they created deep and lasting impressions in Margaret's memory.

Margaret's first-grade year had marked a transition for both her and Louella. Margaret went to school every day and loved it, without giving too much thought to what her mother did during all those hours while she was gone. And why should she have? What child of six is mindful of much beyond the immediate horizon? Most of that year, Louella had walked Margaret to school and then walked back to the school to meet her again at the end of the day.

Margaret knew most of the other kids, even the first graders, walked home with neighbors or older siblings, but she didn't have any of those available, at least none that Louella approved. When Louella came to school each afternoon, Margaret hated it. She chafed in her mother's company as they walked home, and Margaret made sure to let Louella know it, in that way that only daughters can.

The day came, finally, when Margaret was allowed to walk home by herself. The week before, Louella had come only halfway to the school, meeting Margaret on the corner before she would have to cross any streets. When five days passed with no mishap, and with Margaret demonstrating her street-crossing skills adequately, she asked her mother if she could just please walk all the way home by herself. Louella waited a considered moment before answering.

"Okay," Louella said. "You can try it next week. Only one day at a time, though."

Margaret knew this was the only answer she was going to get, but that didn't mean it made sense to her. If she could do it one day, why couldn't she do it every day?

Margaret's first day walking home on her own was a day of true spring sunshine pushing away the chilly April wind. The sun made a hot spot on top of her cropped, brown hair, and her whole being soaked in the new warmth. She walked slowly. She made sure to notice everything.

She stopped and bent down to examine a troop of tiny black ants marching into their sandy little hill in the middle of the cracked sidewalk. Margaret liked the way their bodies moved so rhythmically, so in sync in and out of their hill. Then she looked up from the ants to notice the newly-bloomed, blindingly yellow forsythia, which swagged its way along the sides of almost all the houses down the street as far as she could see.

Margaret walked along a little farther, then stopped again to watch as some of the older kids whizzed by on their bicycles, finally jacketless. She knew it would be a long time before she herself would be allowed to ride her bike back and forth to school. She had gotten a two-wheeler for her birthday in September, and she had practiced on it a lot, up and down their short driveway and sometimes on the choppy stretch of sidewalk in front of their house. Before winter had come and interrupted her riding, Sam had even walked along beside her on a few Saturdays down to the elementary school. Her father had watched and encouraged her in his quiet way as she road smooth, limitless ovals around the empty, newly-paved parking lot. But that freedom was always cut too short because Louella expected them home to take her to the pharmacy, or to the Acme for something she'd forgotten, or to do some other needed errand. Her mother didn't drive.

Margaret continued on her walk home that first day very happily. She stopped at the Stop sign at First Avenue, checking both ways and then checking again, as she had been taught. Then she crossed the street and stepped up onto the sidewalk again, now on her own block. As she got closer to her house, she could glimpse Louella waiting for her out on the small front stoop. Margaret had already pictured her there, watchful. But when she saw her mother waiting there for real, something was out of concert with her buoyant, springtime feeling. The air around Louella fairly snapped. And then Margaret saw, with shock, the long forsythia switch in her mother's hands, just a few blooms still clinging to the stripped branch. The bright yellow, so joyous just moments before, now seemed like a warning. And Margaret's luxurious spring afternoon was turned on its ear, just like that.

Louella had never switched Margaret before, and she didn't that afternoon, either. Maybe she had meant to, and then changed her mind. Maybe her anger had curled itself back into that deep place where it lived once Margaret was on the stoop there in front of her. Or maybe Louella had intended the switch only as a signal, a symbol of potential punishment, and something to grasp in her moments of furious worry. Margaret would never know.

What she did know was that she'd taken entirely too long getting herself home that day. Her new freedom was immediately revoked as she'd known it would be the moment she'd seen Louella's rigid face. When Margaret was finally allowed to walk home without Louella again, she did it without lingering to study the world, and with a new understanding about her mother. Whatever force kept Louella's emotions so tightly controlled, the force that kept the switch stilled in her grasp, also kept her from enjoying or understanding a few thoughtless, free-form moments in the sun.

Twenty-six

The light outside is starting to change as Margaret layers each item carefully back into the cedar chest and closes the lid gently. The morning is almost gone. Compelled by all her sorting through and taking stock, she's decided the rest of the day will be for cleaning out closets, maybe even the basement if she doesn't run out of steam.

Margaret is highly curious about what's in the letter her mother has left for Sarah. What did Louella have to say to her daughter that she didn't want to say out loud, that she didn't want to share with Margaret? All over again, she feels the discomfort and guilt she used to feel watching Louella and Sarah instantly connect with one another. Margaret knows her mother loved her, of course. But Louella's love for Sarah was something more. It was somehow easier, less fraught, unfractured. Margaret was the necessary but then extraneous link between them.

Margaret folds the blanket back into its paper, ties it back up, and then places the bundle into a large shopping bag. It's ready to travel to where it's supposed to be. She will call Sarah later and figure out when would be a good time for a visit.

If only it were that easy for all of us to end up in the right place, where we are meant to be, she thinks. And is that just one place for each of us, or many?

As a child, Margaret always felt like her family was a tribe of three inhabiting their own island. Louella, Sam, and her. Her parents had purposely removed themselves from their roots, relocated to a new place, and begun a new kind of life. Even though her mother came from a large family, they didn't visit their Pennsylvania relatives very often. Louella was too firmly planted in her New Jersey existence.

Louella usually talked on the phone to her own mother, once a week on Sundays. Margaret listened to these Sunday calls from the top of the staircase, not really eavesdropping, but not making her presence obvious, either. During these conversations with Pennsylvania, Louella was pulled into the shape of a woman Margaret only partly recognized, talking about people and places Margaret only knew a little bit. After talking to Gran for a while, Louella always talked to Carrol. When she talked to her brother, her voice and demeanor were different again. Margaret could tell that Carrol was her mother's favorite brother, maybe even her favorite sibling. She always thought Louella talked to Carrol more like she was his mother than his sister. But Louella had been already grown up when Carrol was born, so maybe that was why.

Margaret knew that her mother had been married once before when she was nineteen, which was long before she'd married Sam. She also knew that right around the time Carrol was born, Louella was living back on the farm where she'd grown up, because her first husband had died. Louella was always very vague about this earlier part of her life. It really had nothing to do with Margaret, and she wasn't compelled to ask her mother much about it.

Louella's weekly calls to Pennsylvania always ended after she spoke to Carrol. Then, just as easily as hanging up the phone, she changed right back in to the mother Margaret recognized. She was back on the island.

Unlike Louella, Sam had no one in Pennsylvania to call. He'd been an only child, and his mother, Willetta, had died just after Margaret was born. When Willetta had begun to lose her vision, Margaret's other grandmother, Alma, who she called Gran, offered to have Willetta move to the farm so she wouldn't be by herself. But Willetta, too stubborn for her own good, decided she would rather fall down and die right in her own house than depend on anyone else.

At least that's how Louella phrased it, when it occurred to Margaret to ask why she only had one grandmother. And in the end, that's exactly what had happened. Willetta caught her toe on the fancy runner at the top of her front stairs. Down she went. She broke her neck and died before she ever laid eyes on her only grandchild. Louella described her mother-in-law as a spindly, opinionated, grandiose-acting woman, and Sam didn't temper her description too much. Accordingly, Margaret had always pictured her Purcell grandmother clothed in black, draped in a web-like shawl, with her face in a severe bunch, sort of like a taller, less green Wicked Witch of the West. Even though Margaret knew Willetta had fallen down the stairs, her child's mind imagined this grandmother's death as a shriveling up and crumbling away, like a crust of bread drying out, her final breaths breaking her down into dust.

Even having removed herself to another state, another life, Louella was a responsible woman, a dutiful daughter. When major events occurred, she went, and this meant Margaret went, too.

One childhood visit to Osceola Mills stood out in sharp relief in Margaret's memory against the backdrop of all the others. Gran had died the summer before Margaret turned twelve. Carrol called Louella the night it happened. When the phone rang at almost eleven o'clock, Margaret knew it must be something important, because the phone never rang that late in their house.

Margaret crept out of her bedroom and down the hall to sit at the top of the stairs in her favorite listening spot. With her finger she traced the patterns in the soft, swirly carpet. She knew right away that her mother was talking to Carrol. She heard her mother's questions. How did it happen? Where was she? Then Margaret heard her mother say that they would arrive the following afternoon. The service will be the day after that, Louella asked. What time? In the pauses between her mother's words, Margaret could envision Louella's mouth set in a serious straight line, eyes closed in concentration.

After Louella hung up the phone, Margaret heard her walk into the living room and systematically restate the conversation to Sam. Alma died, this afternoon. The service will be the day after tomorrow. Margaret could also picture her father sitting in his easy chair, listening attentively to Louella with his eyes as well as his ears, as he usually seemed to do. Louella spoke as if the logistics were first and foremost. She barely acknowledged that these details were related to a loss, that her mother was gone.

Of the nine Reams children, five were left. With all their husbands, wives, and children, Margaret had an overflow of aunts, uncles, and cousins to figure out. At the funeral, they were a sea of black inside the hot church, family and neighbors all swaying and sweating together.

Then they stood in the cemetery, dark clothes soaking in and holding close the July sun. Louella and the other women wore dark dresses and small hats with netting over their faces. Margaret wasn't made to wear a hat, and she was relieved. She knew if she'd been any older, her mother would have made her wear one. With her head bowed, she looked up through her lashes at the older girls around her, girls who seemed like a different breed, occupying a place Margaret didn't feel she was even close to at almost twelve. They were all wearing hats, but most of them were wearing lipstick, too. Maybe they liked wearing their hats, Margaret decided. As she considered the gulf between twelve and beyond twelve, Sam stood behind her, his tall frame casting a long shadow and the idea of coolness.

In the dark of the July evening after the service it wasn't any cooler than it had been during the midday heat. Margaret slept, or tried to sleep, in the room she always stayed in when they visited Osceola. But her cot was narrow, with no space to spread out and find the cool places in the sheets like she did in her bed at home.

Each time they stayed overnight, Margaret was amazed knowing that four of Louella's brothers had slept in this tiny room when they were growing up. Margaret was used to her large, unshared bedroom with its spacious bed, writing desk, double bookshelves, and small walk-in cedar closet. To her, the room where she slept in Gran's house seemed more like a closet itself. She was usually comfortable enough in the familiar room, though, even when it was hot. But something had been missing on this visit, shifting her comfort to disquiet.

Louella had always referred to Gran as a brisk, efficient woman with little time or inclination for softness. Yet the grandmother Margaret had known was a woman who had always left a fresh flower waiting for her in a little jam jar of water on the bedside table. Just a wildflower from somewhere around the farm, just a bit of something to let Margaret know Gran thought she was worth the welcome. On this visit, when Margaret brought her bag up to the closet room, the absence of Gran's small gift had carved a new bit of emptiness somewhere inside her.

In the blue-black depth of that sleepless night, Margaret crept down the back staircase leading to the small pantry beside the kitchen. She was bored of trying and failing to sleep, and decided to get a drink of water. The murmur of women's voices drifted under the pantry door, and Margaret waited to open it, listening. She couldn't hear the actual words being traded, but she could feel the tension in between the tones, rigid and strung tight with discord.

Louella was in the kitchen with her sisters, Angelica and Lenore. Margaret knew her mother's relationship with her Aunt Lenore to be easy and affectionate. Margaret's middle name was *Lenore*, after all. But she could remember only a few times Aunt Angelica had even been in Osceola whenever Louella and Margaret were visiting. Margaret had never had a conversation with this aunt beyond the necessary greetings. She hadn't really considered this fact before. There were always so many relatives milling around when she was at Gran's house with her mother.

Louella had explained to Margaret more than once that when you had so many brothers and sisters, you loved them, but could not possible like all of them all the time. As an only child, Margaret condemned her mother for not embracing the simple luck of having all these siblings, love them or not. Oh, to have someone to bicker with, to choose to like or not like them, even as you loved them through blood and obligation. Margaret had been a self-contained child from the start, but would she have been different if it hadn't just been her? Louella was always quick to emphasize how lucky Margaret was, how rich. She had quiet space, uninterrupted time, plenty to eat, clothes that were not handed down or made over. According to Louella, Margaret's life was full of luxury. Margaret was always quick to retort that she wished she did have someone to share with, even to fight with. When she slung these comments at her mother, heavy and targeted, Louella's only response was silence and then walking away.

But that late night as Margaret listened from her hidden place in the pantry, the tension between her mother and Angelica seemed weighted with a different kind of fierceness. The two sisters were like the repelling ends of two magnets, pressing and squeezing the air between them, building pressure without ever making contact. Even though she couldn't make out the words being traded, in her stillness Margaret felt like she could almost reach out and touch it, that bitter, unfamiliar energy pushing into the hot air of the kitchen.

Now, so many years later, Margaret holds the rediscovered blanket on her lap and thinks about that sad, sweltering day of her grandmother's funeral, and the feeling of that night in the pantry. She decides that when Sarah's daughter is old enough to visit overnight, she will resurrect Gran's flower tradition, even though Margaret realizes that in the end it may mean nothing to her granddaughter. She tries to brush this thought away, but she can't ignore what she's learned as the mother of an adult daughter. Sarah's insights and revelations have taught Margaret that mothers are not the memory makers they often think themselves to be. Margaret knows now how many of her own most poignant moments were released easily from Sarah's grasp, while those memories that were mere wisps to Margaret herself are entrenched in Sarah's heart and mind as legend.

Twenty-seven

Louella was there with Margaret when Sarah was born. Not in the room, but just outside, sitting squarely on a molded plastic hospital chair, her still slim legs crossed at the ankle, every muscle waiting. Sam sat in the chair next to her, watching her wait.

Louella and Sam didn't visit Margaret and John very often. Margaret hadn't been sure if her mother would come when the baby was born, or if she even wanted Louella there. A piece of Margaret wished for Louella's predictable, familiar presence. Her mother had listened well, better than Margaret had expected, through all the painful years of wanting and waiting for a baby. Margaret's need for her mother's attention during this wishing time surprised her. But then Margaret was finally pregnant, her uncharacteristic and naked neediness filled. She and Louella returned to their customary positions, which meant Margaret didn't ask her mother for anything, and Louella, in return, tried not to ask too many questions or offer unsolicited advice.

When the time came, Margaret didn't have to decide if she would ask Louella to come or not, because her mother just showed up. A week before her due date, Margaret's doctor thought there might be a problem with the baby's umbilical cord, and he decided they shouldn't wait to find out. He told Margaret to go home, pack her bag, and come to the hospital. They would induce labor the following morning. Far from being panicked, that plan sounded just fine to Margaret. It created a scenario that presented childbirth as a controlled and structured process, which appealed to her much more than the unpredictability of her water breaking in someplace like the grocery store.

The afternoon before Sarah was born, Margaret was completely, inwardly focused. She unpacked and repacked the overnight bag she'd had ready for several weeks. She slowly and carefully ate a plain chicken breast and roll, just as the nurse had suggested as she was leaving her obstetrician's office. Somehow, in the last few hours before going to the hospital, Margaret forgot about the decision she'd been weighing for weeks. To call her mother or not call her?

John called Louella though, and she and Sam arrived at the hospital in the middle of the following morning, just as the Pitocin took Margaret in its throttling grip. Margaret talked to her mother about many things while Louella held her hand and wiped her forehead and fed her ice chips. But even just hours later, Margaret couldn't remember any of it. She'd been riding a flowing, endless river of pain, with only slight crests and dips the whole way through. Whatever she and Louella may have said to each other during those hours of pain did not stick, would not live anywhere in Margaret's accessible memory. And after it was all over, she never thought to ask her mother about what she might have missed.

When it was time to push at last, Margaret's body knew it and seemed to know how to do it, even as she still surged along the rushing current of her pain. John took his place at Margaret's side as the nurses ushered Louella out of the room. Margaret does remember the way Louella looked as she walked out, this image an independent imprint from that day. Her mother's face became that of a much younger woman, and it wore a mixture of clear joy and loss, all at once.

Did Louella feel in that moment like she was losing her daughter? Would Margaret someday feel that exact loss herself? Louella had never been sentimental. She'd endured enough general upheaval and loss in her lifetime to boil the emotion out of the softest of souls. Margaret thought her parents' marriage was happy. She thought she had been a wanted child, even if not a planned one, so late in her parents' lives. But she didn't really know any of these things for sure, not in a way she could have articulated. None of them talked about feelings very often. And besides, daughters don't always see what lies along the delicate and intricate inner seams of who their mothers are and were.

Margaret would grow to wonder, at every stage, what Sarah really thought of her, if her daughter saw her as she saw herself. How did you let your daughter know you truly and also preserve something of who you were yourself, separate from who you were as a mother?

Louella came back into the room several hours later, after Sarah was out of Margaret's body and warm in her arms. The grief Margaret thought she'd seen on her mother's face was gone, and she found only joy there. This Louella was someone new, a woman Margaret had never seen before. She was a grandmother now.

Louella held out her arms and Margaret passed Sarah into them. She had no idea what to say to her mother, so she said nothing at all.

"Oh, Margaret," was all Louella herself managed to say. But in that unmarred moment, they needed no other words.

Twenty-eight

As a child, it had always been obvious to Margaret that Louella was the one in charge of their tribe, their island. Sam went to work, and Louella ran the household, but in their family it seemed like more than the traditional division of labor somehow. Louella wasn't overbearing or demanding or headstrong, and she didn't need delicate handling either. The difference was more in the way that Sam raised her up. Louella was the lookout. She charted their course. From her tower, she surveyed the surrounding land of their small world, mapped their place in it, and determined how far toward the edges it was safe to roam. Sam had his own attributes. He was thoughtful and inquisitive, pondering and inventive. But Louella was the one in charge. No matter how her parents themselves defined things, Margaret knew this to be true. And she also knew that if Louella were ever to lose her bearings, falter in the tower, they might all come crashing down.

During her senior year in high school, Margaret was chosen as the editor in chief of the school newspaper, and she spent many concentrated hours in the basement newspaper office. One night, Sam came to get her there, and he was not himself, not the reticent, thoughtful father she lived with. It was like an aggressive stranger had possessed the tall, patient frame of her father. Margaret was working there with two of the junior editors. When Sam opened the door into the dim basement room with enough force to slam it back against the inside wall, all three of them whipped their heads up in unison from the galley page they were studying. Sam looked right through the other two to Margaret and barked her name.

"Dad," was all she replied.

He'd never been in the newspaper office. Margaret couldn't remember a time Sam had ever sought her out at school before. How had he known where to find her? Margaret had no precedent for her response. It would have been too many words to ask what Sam was doing there and how he'd even known where she would be and why he looked so unlike himself.

"You needed to be home an hour ago," Sam said loudly. "It's Thursday night."

He was correct. It was Thursday. Usually, Margaret stayed late after school to work on the newspaper on Wednesdays, sometimes not getting home until past dinnertime. But it was the week after Easter, school had been closed on Monday, and everything in the weekly schedule was off by one.

Except the Acme. Thursday was their grocery shopping night because Thursday night was the only night the grocery story was open. Louella, Sam, and Margaret always went to the store together. As Margaret got older, sometimes she fulfilled this obligation cheerfully, sometimes moodily, but she always went.

For goodness sake, she thought, as Sam stood still staring at her, waiting for an answer, or maybe an apology. Couldn't they have gone without me, just this one time? Better yet, couldn't her mother just learn to drive already?

Louella had never had a driver's license, a fact which she dismissed fluidly as an inconsequential detail. But the fact that Louella didn't drive was of every consequence to Margaret. Every other mother she knew drove. Driving was no big deal, Margaret thought. Sam had even offered to teach her to drive over the summer. Margaret had always had to walk everywhere or rely on someone else's mother to drive her when the weather was bad, or it was too far, or Sam wasn't home. Wasn't her mother embarrassed by that? It embarrassed Margaret to always need a ride but never give one. Sometimes it was easier to just not go somewhere than to ask for a ride. Then Margaret would stay home, resentful and disdainful, wallowing in her choice.

Margaret gave Sam's glare right back to him, but this proved ineffective. She turned to the other kids with a scowling shrug.

"I guess I have to go. You'll have to finish this up for tomorrow without me," she spat out.

Then she picked up her school books and notebooks from their pile on the corner table, clenching them forcefully to her chest. As Margaret moved past her father and out the door, Sam maintained his steely stare. She stalked up the cement steps and out into the parking lot. Margaret knew she was being disrespectful, something she didn't feel driven to very often with Sam. But he was behind her, and she didn't have to look him in the eye.

"Why did you have to come get me?" she asked once they were both seated in the car. "I had a lot of work to finish up in there."

Margaret was leading her class and would probably graduate in June as valedictorian. Then she would be going to Douglass College to study journalism. In just a few months, she would be sixty miles and a world away from Haddon Heights. She would be freed from Thursday night grocery shopping forever. But not yet, and she knew it. Sam knew it, too. As he turned to her to answer her question, he became more like her real, regular father again, though he was still upset.

"She misses you. And she's only going to miss you more," he said quietly. "You should have come home."

"I know," Margaret answered, and with this admission came the release of all her huffed-up resentment.

Louella had been having a difficult year. What Sam labeled that night as loneliness over Margaret's impending departure probably had as much or more to do with what she was already missing. Over the winter, after being sick for only a few months, their neighbor, Carlotta, had died. Carlotta had been Louella's closest friend, her only friend, really. Without her, Louella was adrift in a way Sam and Margaret had never witnessed.

Carlotta's husband, Sal, began coming over to their house for dinner on Mondays and Fridays. When Carlotta was alive, the Purcells had almost always been the visitors at the Serchia's house, not the other way around. So those Monday and Friday dinners could have been stilted and sad, but instead they seemed like a true comfort to both Sal and Louella. Yet on those evenings, when it was time for Sal to go back home, time for Margaret's family to resume its familiar form, Margaret could feel the warmth of the shared mealtime leave the house as Sal left.

Louella's grief was easy for Margaret to disregard most of the time, both because of their habitual lack of sharing and because she was enclosed in the capsule of her teenage world. Margaret was so anxious to launch off into her own separate life that she didn't think too much about how her leaving might siphon off even more of her mother's spirit. And really, it's not a child's role to think that way. Children are not, and shouldn't be, able to understand how their growing up and growing away causes their mothers pain. Losing a child in this inevitable way isn't tragic, but just as truly felt. When your children grow up and away from you, as you watch their small, innocent outlines dissolve into the grownup figures you've always dreamed of them becoming, you mourn even as you rejoice.

When Sam caught glimpses of this impending loss coursing around and through Louella, knowing what she had already lost, it undid him. That Thursday night so long ago, it had turned him into a man Margaret didn't recognize as he slammed his way into the school basement.

Twenty-nine

Sarah had always been an emotional girl, hyper-aware of feelings and interactions around her, not the *what* of a situation, but the *how*. Her perception went beyond generic empathy or sensitivity. Sarah seemed to tune immediately and almost exclusively to the emotional center of any experience or exchange. This can be an asset, being this heightened. But, especially in a young child, it's also a burden, this inability to shed someone else's skin or escape from under the perceived weight of the world.

Sarah was six years old the first time Margaret recognized how overwhelmed her daughter could become without much warning, the triggers imperceptible to Margaret until after the storm. They were in church on a late autumn Sunday, which wasn't where they usually spent their Sunday mornings.

Margaret hadn't gone to church at all growing up. Everyone else's family did, it seemed, so she'd always felt like this was one more detail of so many that made her different from every other kid she knew. If she was ever asked where she went to church, she had a made-up answer ready. To her cousins' church and then to their house for a big family dinner. That was Margaret's prepared reply even though nobody really cared as much about her answer as Margaret did.

Margaret knew her mother sometimes visited St. Augustine, the Catholic church down the block from their house. She'd heard Carlotta say something once to Louella about the priest having seen Louella there. Her mother wasn't Catholic. Why did she go there? Margaret wanted to know. Or, if Louella wanted to go there so much, why didn't she take Margaret with her? Why did she keep this experience all for herself? Margaret knew lots of kids who complained about having to sit through Sunday services, but she was curious. Her mother's going to church without her was just one more aspect of Louella that didn't make sense to Margaret, that didn't include her, that separated them. And because of this, even when she was still just a child herself, Margaret decided that when she was a mother, she would take her children to church.

Sometimes she managed to do it. But John worked such long hours at his law firm, and then usually right through Saturdays at home. Sundays felt like the only family time they really had. Sometimes it felt right to get up and out and go to church together. More often, it seemed right to spend the morning hours still in their pajamas eating pancakes or heading out for a long walk in the state park near their house. As a kid, John had gone regularly to a Dutch Reformed church, but he confessed that what he remembered most was slyly spit balling his younger brother with wadded up gum wrappers. He much preferred pancakes and hiking.

That autumn Sunday when Sarah was six, John had stayed home, and it was just the two of them, mother and daughter. Margaret glanced down at Sarah sitting next to her as the organ introduction swelled and everyone rose to sing the first hymn. Moments before, Sarah had been smiling and doodling funny faces on her bulletin. But now she sat very still, head bowed, her eyes pinched with the effort to control the tide of tears washing down her beautiful, flushed face. Margaret's heart constricted as she sat back down next to Sarah. She put a firm arm around her and squeezed just a little. Sarah was unaware of her mother, submerged, dragged down by an undertow of emotion released by the music. This mighty force was so foreign to Margaret, especially in someone so intimately familiar to her. Despite how totally undone Sarah was by it, it intrigued Margaret. She studied Sarah separately, dispassionately, even as she comforted her. And Margaret never forgot that moment.

Thirty

When Margaret is finished sorting through all the upstairs closets, she decides to skip the hall coat closet and move on to the basement. As she walks down the basement stairs, she's confronted with the colorful remains of Sarah's childhood. Elementary school artwork still lines both walls of the stairwell. Margaret doesn't go down to the basement much anymore, and even when she does, she usually skims right past the stick figures and tissue paper mosaics, the handprint turkeys, the cotton ball snowmen. Always intent on the task at hand.

But not today. Today she pauses and studies all of it. She thinks about what kind of mother Sarah will be. Which parts of the script handed down to her will she follow closely, which ones will she adapt, and which ones will she flatly reject? How will Sarah treasure and preserve all the handprint turkeys coming her way?

Louella's approach to motherhood had been laissez faire. Luckily, Margaret was a self-starter, ready and eager to launch, very motivated if she liked something. She loved school and excelled in every subject without it seeming like too much work. She had learned to read fluidly by the time she was five, and then she'd read every book she could get her hands on, some of them two or three times over. She especially liked to pore over the heavy volumes of the Encyclopedia Britannica that lined the built-in shelves of their living room. She loved to tap dance. She loved to experiment in the kitchen, but only when Louella was in the mood to give her some space and not hover over her. Margaret found her own way toward the things she wanted to try but without any pressure or suggestion from her mother.

This was the reason Margaret never really learned to swim. She was strenuously against swimming. She had no interest in flinging her body from its usual warm, dry environment into the cold wet of any pool, lake, or ocean. The threat of polio was rampant during the summers of her early childhood, providing valid support for Margaret's disdain for swimming, and Louella, true to form, did not make her.

Then, during the summer before seventh grade, the swimming issue resurfaced. Margaret's friend, Karen, who had moved in three houses down in the middle of their second-grade year, was going to sleep away camp for two weeks that July, and Margaret decided she wanted to go with her. Margaret had never spent any extended time away from home, and Louella seemed surprised that she wanted to go to camp for so long, two whole weeks. But after some deliberating and Louella checking with Karen's parents, Margaret was told she could go.

Karen had been to this camp the previous two summers and talked about it a lot, so Margaret knew there would be a swimming test, which you had to pass to even be in your bathing suit and get close to the water during swimming time. To pass the test, she would have to swim across the pool using whichever stroke she chose and then tread water for one minute. Margaret only did things when she was pretty sure she'd be good at them, without too much floundering. She didn't even attempt the swimming test. She knew she wouldn't be able to perform at even the rudimentary level required. Her early dislike for the water was by then a palpable fear.

For those two weeks at camp, Margaret sat on the lake beach far back from the water's edge at swimming time. For an hour each morning and again each afternoon, she sweated through her clothes and swatted at black flies as she watched everyone else in her squad splash and dive and laugh. She was the only non-swimmer that year. She was frustrated by the thick stubbornness that had kept her from at least trying to learn to swim. Margaret could barely admit even to herself the depth of her fear, the breadth of her humiliation. All of it settled its weight upon her in the shape of anger at Louella. Why hadn't she forced Margaret to learn to swim, like a better mother would have? Why didn't she make Margaret do anything?

That was probably why Margaret turned out to be just the opposite way with Sarah.

"Grandma never made you do anything, and now you make me do everything!"

Sarah flung this accusation at Margaret on a regular basis. It became her protest mantra as Margaret insisted she take hold of any and every opportunity, and follow them all through to the bitter end, because Margaret *was not raising a quitter*. Margaret especially pushed Sarah to do things that made her feel unsure and out of her element.

Being a mother is such a universal and simultaneously isolating experience. Feeling the way along its winding, frequently forked, constantly uphill path, that path leading right into the thicket was frightening. When to insist, when to give guidance, when to feign turning away?

Margaret thought later, once Sarah was grown up, that her tendency to push Sarah so much was compounded by having wanted and waited for a child for so long. To make sure she did her job well, and to make certain she wasn't like Louella, she thrust Sarah headlong out into the world every day, in every way. Her sense of parental responsibility was rewarded by what she recognized as Sarah's ability to tolerate a steeper learning curve than Margaret herself was ever able to handle gracefully.

When Sarah was three, Margaret had enrolled her in a preschool swimming class, a clear attempt to rectify Louella's greatest failing. Margaret desperately wanted Sarah to be a good swimmer, to not be afraid of the water. This was the one essential tool Margaret felt was missing from her own skill set. She watched as Sarah learned to leap into the deep water and swim surely into the arms of her waiting instructor. Arms that were not Margaret's arms. She was both relieved by and envious of this truth.

Fortunately, Sarah loved the water at age three and forever after. Watching Sarah swim as a child, Margaret wished she could feel that kind of disembodiment. But she was again the girl on that glaring lake beach at summer camp. Her stubbornness and fear, her need for control, had always been bigger than all her wishing.

Sarah took every kind of swimming lesson Margaret could find, then stroke clinics and junior lifesaving. She swam, she dove, she snorkeled. She abandoned herself, body and soul, to the power of the water without hesitation, dissolving completely into its liquid freedom.

She even learned to scuba dive with John when they went to the Caribbean on a spring break trip when Sarah was fifteen. When she surfaced after their first few minutes, Sarah insisted that Margaret see some of the beauty she and her father were seeing underwater. Margaret pushed her fear aside just long enough to strap on a mask and rest her face on the surface of the water. While she gripped the side of the boat desperately, trading easy breath for just a glimpse, Sarah breathed under there, fluidly at one with the fish.

Sarah

Thirty-one

Sarah learned to swim in the chilly aqua waters of the local Y pool. She's surprised how clear the memory is now, so many years later. She had launched herself into the deep with sheer joy, without hesitation.

Then there were years of swimming lessons, learning all the strokes, learning to dive in the perfect arc, joining the summer swim team. Her mother signed her up for everything. The culmination of it all was junior lifesaving at Pilgrim Lake on Cape Cod, the summer Sarah was twelve. Sarah loved being in the lake, but she did not want to take lifesaving. That was for lifeguards, and she did not want to be a lifeguard. Cool as they were in their red Guard suits, twirling their whistle lanyards, she just didn't want to be part of their pack. They spent way too much time watching other people in the water, and Sarah only wanted to be in it for herself.

Margaret was immutable. The lifesaving course was mandatory, not because Margaret herself had done it, but because she had not. Margaret's justification for never learning to swim was her own mother's less-is-more approach to child raising. According to Margaret, Louella had never made her do anything she didn't want to do. This seemed to make Margaret approach mothering as an act of defiance. Did most women consciously choose to mother in perfect parallel or direct opposition to how they were mothered themselves, as a way to balance out the universe?

But Sarah had known it was more than lack of interest keeping Margaret on the side of the pool. Her mother was truly afraid of the water. Even at age three, that first day at the Y, Sarah could feel an unfamiliar rigidness clamping all her mother's movements and encouragements as they stepped from the steamy close air of the locker room onto the cold, slippery pool deck. Even though she didn't understand it, didn't feel it herself, she'd known this was fear.

Soon, Sarah will be the mother of a daughter herself. She imagines the altering experience of motherhood as a pendulum, like the giant pendulum she'd seen at the Franklin Institute in Philadelphia on a field trip with her third grade Brownie troop. It hung from the ceiling stories above, swinging hypnotically, sweeping the floor, seeming to sweep the whole building. It was mesmerizing. You could imagine you saw the instant the tip reached that lowest point in the middle of its inverted arc, that it paused there for just a breath. Didn't it? But you'd be wrong. It was just a trompe l'oeil, a trick of the eye, a mirage. It never stopped moving.

Sarah thinks motherhood might be like this, a continuing quest to see and seize the moment of equilibrium, while also knowing you're powerless to slow the arc long enough to grab anything. You can only try to recognize the instant of perfect balance for what it is as you pass through it, as it passes through you.

Sarah had finally given up the fight with Margaret over taking, or not taking, junior lifesaving. For two long weeks, she got up early and was on the beach shivering before the sun could warm the grey-green lake water. She learned how to drag people to safety using the underarm hold. She mastered rescue breathing. She plunged into the lake fully clothed in her jeans and heaviest sweatshirt just to disrobe, tie the legs of her jeans together, and then blow them up into a makeshift life vest. That was the last challenge. Then she was finished. Free. Sarah had hated almost every minute of that class, but then for the rest of that summer she reveled in the freedom of not being in it.

She had gained back the gift of the water, and all she wanted to do was swim. She was a dolphin, a seal, a mermaid, lady of the lake, sprite of the sea. A few years earlier, John had gotten them a small motorboat. Out on the bay with her father, Sarah would ride as far forward on the bow as she was allowed, and when the boat was at its fastest, she became the figurehead, at one with her ship. At the same time, she was at one with the water. A small and tender part of Sarah truly believed that if she were to let go and soar overboard, she would be able to breathe under there. She would become part of the sea and just swim away.

Now, waiting for her baby to be born, Sarah bends her days around the rhythms of her body, and the body within. Just like the rhythms of the ocean, her hours are sometimes slow, sometimes fierce with energy.

Sarah started her maternity leave a few weeks early, after two trips to the hospital with pre-term contractions. She already knows she's not going back to work after the baby is born. She can't imagine handing her new little daughter over to anyone else. Sarah's husband, Gavin, works long, late hours and is on the road a lot. They had agreed early on that it would make sense for all of them, for what was to be their family, if Sarah left her job to take care of the baby. And they've figured out that if they're careful, which they are about most things, they can just about make the money work.

Sarah is as sure of this decision as she can be right now, still pregnant, even as she jokes about whether they will still afford take-out pizza on Friday nights. Who really needs pizza? But she can't really know at all how this seismic shift will change the shape her days, change who she is. She swings wildly from overjoyed to overwhelmed. No matter how universal motherhood is, and even with an extra person inside her, most of the time she feels very alone.

Each morning after breakfast, Sarah drives to the gym to use the pool. It's early for her but late for anyone else who swims before work, and she's usually the only one there. The captive air around the pool is always heavy with humidity and chlorine, uncomfortably close, and her bathing suit presses tightly against her. She walks slowly to the edge of the pool, careful not to slip on the slick tiles. She lowers herself down until she's sitting on the side of the deep end. She slides almost soundlessly, feet first, into the cooling water.

In the water. This is the only time Sarah still feels truly like herself. She still loves being underwater best, just like she did as a child. Under the silent weight of the deep, she cannot sense where she ends, and the rest of the world begins. She is in the womb again, floating as her baby floats, untouched.

Thirty-two

Sarah's next-door-neighbor, Lida, is a medium. A *mystic*. Lida is also a typical wife and mother, a lot like Sarah's other neighbors. She goes to the store and comes home with the back of her Subaru wagon loaded with groceries. She hangs sheets on her clothes line if the weather is sunny. She chases her three-year-old, Patrick, around their backyard, squirting his little round body with a hose as he squeals and leaps.

As she moves through all these usual motions in the physical world, Lida wears a mantle of unwavering confidence that sets her apart. She is clear-eyed about what she knows, those things everyone else wonders about or ignores. It's almost like only a small piece of Lida is going about her daily tasks, living her everyday life, while the rest of her floats above, witnessing the expansive ebb and flow of the whole connected universe. And it doesn't seem to matter to Lida at all if anyone else believes what she sees, what she feels, what she says. How reassuring that must be, Sarah thinks, yet also how exhausting.

Throughout Sarah's pregnancy, she's had a nagging feeling of something important left unfinished or unconsidered. Maybe all first-time mothers felt this way.

How would she know? But Lida has picked up on it too, making Sarah feel both validated and worried.

"How are you *feeling?*" Lida asks Sarah more than once with a probing emphasis as they chat over the fence between their two backyards.

"You should come see me," she says.

Sarah knows Lida means for more than a neighborly visit, and Sarah decides yes, she will make a real appointment with Lida.

Sarah decides not to tell Gavin. It's not a lie, not exactly. Just a temporary omission. Gavin and Sarah approach the world very differently. Gavin is all salt, elemental. He deals with his world on a concrete, practical level. See it, hear it, touch it, taste it. Sarah decides it will be better to wait until after the reading to tell him, because then she'll have something more to tell, even if it's only a good story. So, when Gavin notices her scatteredness the night before, she blames the heat, her pregnancy, physical things he will understand and accept.

Sarah functions more instinctively than Gavin, directed more by her gut than logic. She's structured when she needs to be, but it's only her organizational response to living in an uncontrollable world. Isn't every institution – government, religion, even housekeeping – just an attempt to throw reins around the chaos? Aren't they all illusory, temporary?

It's what lies beneath that's making Sarah anxious. How am I going to be someone's mother? There's so much I don't know about ... everything, she thinks. How is she supposed to explain it all and make the world right for a child? Or at least convince her daughter that as the mother she can always solve what needs to be solved. Or that mothers can't fix everything, that living in the face of uncertainty is really the only option we're given.

On the appointed morning, Sarah climbs Lida's front steps heavily. The weather is already hot for May, but Sarah is chilled and breathless with anticipation. She has resolved to keep her imagination wide open, to recognize this experience as subjective and personal. A time for feelings, not facts. She hopes at least she will leave more settled than she is now, more serene. More like Lida herself always seems to be.

Sarah has been into Lida's house a few times for a cup of coffee, a glass of wine, a borrowed egg. But this time is different. She realizes she has expectations without wanting to. What if the whole process turns out to be anticlimactic? What if it's a repeat of the only palm reading she's ever had, by a heavily tattooed woman one lazy, sixteen-year-old summer afternoon in New Hope? That day she was granted the standard long life, endless love, and great happiness. What if Lida's pronouncements are equally rote? Then it will be a friend bearing the weight of Sarah's disappointment.

Sarah pulls in a deep breath, exhales, and knocks decisively. Lida comes right to the door. Her glossy black hair snakes in a long braid all the way down to her waist. Her eyes, upturned and intelligent, are dark under even darker brows. Her smooth, pale face is almost unnaturally unmarked. Garnet beads drip from her ears, and she wears a flowing, dark blue skirt shot through with scarlet. Sarah has never seen this particular skirt before, but it isn't a costume. Lida is almost always dressed in something flowing. It's difficult to tell what shape she really is underneath.

"Sarah, I'm so glad you're here."

Lida's soft voice flows around Sarah and pulls her through the door into the front hallway. Little Patrick stands at Lida's side, clutching a piece of her skirt while her hand rests lightly on the top of his head. His black hair is identical to Lida's. He's a little bit shy sometimes. The wild, laughing child Sarah usually sees tripping around the backyard is tucked away inside a hesitant smile today. A college-age girl wearing cutoff jeans and a faded grey tee shirt steps through the sliding door into the dining room at the back of the house.

"C'mon, Patrick," she says. "Let's go swing."

Lida gently smooths the hair off Patrick's forehead. She caresses his cheek. He smiles up at her more broadly than he had been smiling at Sarah. Then he runs to his babysitter, and together they disappear back through the sliding door. Sarah watches and wonders. Will she caress her child's soft cheek that way someday? Will she feel that way about the child she has not yet laid eyes on? She's certain she will, but this certainty blankets her with a feeling she can't define. She remembers there's some saying about having a child and your heart walking around outside of your body forever after?

Lida leads Sarah through the hallway and downstairs to the basement, which turns out to be not like a basement at all. As Sarah walks down the stairs, she smells incense and sees soft light sliding in through the high windows. Shimmery gold cloth drapes across the ceiling. Sarah follows Lida into a small, dark room with cushions on the floor and a large, velvety armchair in one corner. Sarah assumes Lida will sit in the chair, and she worries about how she's going to get herself down to the floor and then back up again. But, without speaking, Lida gestures for Sarah to take the chair, and she sits herself down on the floor on a large, floral pillow.

Sinking into the soft chair, Sarah breathes slowly and tries to relax. In that moment, Sarah feels, urgently, the need to know what Lida senses about her marriage, about the baby on the way, about the kind of mother Sarah is going to be. She wants to know if all the pieces that cement her daily existence are as enduring as she believes them to be.

Lida opens her mouth and begins to speak. She does not answer any of the questions Sarah might have thought to ask. She doesn't confirm any of Sarah's beliefs, or allay any of her doubts. Instead, Lida offers Sarah her grandmother, Louella.

Thirty-three

As an only child of middle class suburbia, Sarah had tried to imagine what it must have been like to have eight brothers and sisters all crammed together in a small farmhouse. She knew this was the way her grandmother had grown up. Sarah also knew Louella's diligence and natural curiosity had propelled her from the small school in Osceola to the regional high school at the early age of twelve. The fluidity of this approach clashed with Sarah's structured experiences. Who went to high school at the age of twelve?

Beyond the facts of Louella's childhood, Sarah also knew her grandmother had been married once before. Her first husband had died, she had married Sam, and Margaret had been born. Sarah had never asked Louella very much about the earlier parts of her adult life. Those details were immaterial to who Louella was to Sarah. In Sarah's mind, Louella was a little girl on an Pennsylvania farm running around with all those brothers and sisters, a little girl Sarah sometimes pretended to be herself. Or Louella was just Grandma, lumpy and soft, with hair the color and texture of baby mouse fur, with skin like old, loved velvet. For Sarah, there had never been any other version in between these two Louellas.

Back in her own house, Sarah's visit to Lida feels like it was days ago, not hours. That deep, dark basement room had been another realm. In it, Sarah had seen everything around her and within her through a new lens. She'd felt the air around her move and press with new meaning.

She paces slowly on her screened porch, waiting for her mother to answer the phone. She's restless, even with the weight of a pregnant belly, even though the day has gotten even hotter and more humid since she climbed Lida's steps this morning.

Sarah feels like she has something delicate and fragile to offer. She wants to talk to Margaret, needs to talk to her mother. At the same time Sarah is afraid that talking about her experience will shatter it like an eggshell until it is recognizable but ruined. Worthless. Dead.

Once, when Sarah was six or seven, visiting her grandparents overnight, she and Louella had investigated a robin's nest as they poked around in the backyard. It was nestled in the branches of a pretty tree, low to the ground and covered with magenta flowers against broad, glossy leaves. Louella had already known the nest was there. She walked Sarah over to see it, hoping they would also see the babies chirping hungrily away. But they were all gone.

"We missed them. They must have learned to fly, just since yesterday," Louella had said.

A few fragments of bright blue shell still lay scattered inside, but that was all. Louella poked her index finger sadly around the empty nest.

"Don't worry," Sarah had reassured her grandmother. "I've seen baby birds in a nest before at home. Besides, they're supposed to fly away. That's how it works."

"Yes," Louella said. "I know they fly away. They all do."

And with that, she had picked up each piece of beautiful, broken shell from the nest, one by one, and put them gently in the pocket of her housedress.

Sarah has told Margaret about Lida, who she is and what she does. But she hadn't told her mother she was going to have a reading. She's not sure how Margaret will react.

Margaret is a minister, spiritual in a necessary way, in her own way. Sarah's mother wasn't always a minister, though this designation is only a recent milestone. Margaret went back to school when Sarah left for college. She fits this new role well, Sarah thinks, and she tries to admire her mother's new path, this new dimension, Margaret's drive to seek a new and untapped part of herself. But still, deep down, this ministerial figure doesn't quite sync with the practical, methodical mother Sarah has always known.

Now we're about to trade places, exchange roles, my mother and I, Sarah thinks. For so long, Margaret was always there, always at the ready, whenever Sarah needed something. Sarah admits to herself that she's still a little disoriented when she calls, and her mother isn't home. She knows this is selfish. Why should Margaret be there, with no one to be there for? She has work to do and people to take care of out there in the world. Sick people, worried people, aging people, hurt people.

But today, Margaret picks up on the fifth ring. Relief and nervousness flood through Sarah at the sound of her mother's voice.

"Hi, sweetie. I was cleaning out closets and even the basement." She sounds a little out of breath.

"Hi," Sarah says back. She's a little bit breathless herself.

"How are you feeling?" The standard question for a pregnant daughter.

"Fine, good... I have to tell you what I did today."

"Oh? What?"

Sarah pictures Margaret with the white phone in her left hand, winding its long pigtailed cord around the fingers of her right. In her mind's eye, her mother sits down on the Windsor chair that's always pulled up to the little desk at the end of her kitchen counter. Sarah stops pacing and sits down in her old wicker chair, a relic from her childhood bedroom that now lives on their porch. She rests her elbows on her knees, her feet planted wide apart.

"I went to my friend Lida's today. For a reading."

"Oh? What did she say?" Sarah hears Margaret's tone become more intent.

"Well, lots of things. It was very interesting. I talked to her about Grandma."

Sarah pauses then, hesitates just for a second. Would asking Margaret questions about her own mother be like kneading a sore muscle, both painful and relieving? Or would it be more like scouring a wound, just painful?

Another "oh," is all Margaret offers into the silence.

Sarah plunges ahead, hoping she won't upset Margaret too much by talking about Louella. She describes sitting in Lida's basement room, the soft light and the mysterious, wandering music. She tells her mother about how Louella was there, really there, about how even though Sarah had a hard time melding herself fully with the otherness of the experience, it hadn't seemed to matter. Louella had very pointedly called Lida's attention to a knitted item, or something made of yarn, that she wanted Sarah to have for the baby. It seemed to be something very important, vital, meant to be passed down. The whole experience, Sarah told Margaret, had been much more concrete and specific than anything Sarah had expected.

"I told Lida I would have to ask you about it. She seemed very definite."

Sarah pauses. She isn't even sure whom she means. Who had been definite? Lida? Louella?

"Well I'll be damned," says the minister. It's a whisper of recognition.

"Do you know what she could have been talking about?" Sarah asks.

"Yes, I do know. I know exactly," says Margaret.

The eggshell has not shattered. It has not been crushed as Sarah feared it might be. It's still intact. It's beautiful, believable.

Margaret starts talking fast, her words tripping over themselves in their haste to be recognized. Sarah pictures her mother standing back up now, her free hand perched on her hip, her phone hand gripping the receiver tightly. Their conversation was not for sitting down anymore. Sarah stands back up, too.

"I was going through the cedar chest just this morning, before I started cleaning out closets," Margaret proceeds. "Do you remember that blanket Grandma had? The white one, with the roses all over it? She made it right before I was born. You might not remember it. You were little when she wrapped it up and put it away. She said it was for you when you had a baby one day. I remembered it last night and decided to get it out this morning. I know how much you love old things, and I thought since the baby's room is going to be red it might end up being kind of pretty in there. It's made of yarn, and it's from Grandma, and she meant for you to have it when you had a baby. Isn't that astounding?"

Sarah exhales heavily, feeling like Margaret has consumed all of her own air and Sarah's, too. Yes, she is astounded.

"Sarah," Margaret says, seemingly unfazed, reeling her daughter back into the moment. "Do you want me to come down over the weekend? To bring the blanket to you?"

They agree to a time on Sunday afternoon, say goodbye, and hang up. As she lowers herself back down into the wicker chair, Sarah imagines Margaret returning to her closet cleaning with extra vigor. She crosses her legs up under her swollen belly, rests her hands, palms up, on her knees. She sits and swirls through little girl memories, granddaughter memories. She comes to rest on the question of whether she is still a granddaughter, when her grandmother is so long gone.

Thirty-four

When Sarah visited Louella, she was allowed to get out of
bed when the birds started chirping. Their morning
songs were the only alarm clock in Louella's house. Sarah
would walk down the carpeted hallway to check in her
grandmother's room. Sometimes Louella was there
waiting for her, sometimes she was already down in the
kitchen.

After breakfast, they would step out the kitchen door
together onto the little linoleum-floored stoop and then
down the steps to the grass. They would scatter the yard
with crusts and crumbled loaf ends. The takers were
mostly robins, or at least that's how Sarah remembers it.
They were common birds, not enchanting, not bright or
beautiful, not rare. They were a solidifying, constant piece
of the backyard tableau, ordinary in every good way.

The house on Crest Avenue contained the world
during those visits. Since Louella didn't drive,
grandmother and granddaughter were housebound
together. Sarah could remember only a handful of times
Sam drove them to the Acme to get a few groceries, and
once when they'd gone to play miniature golf and get ice
cream, but that was when Margaret was with them, too.
Sarah realized as she got older that her visits to her
grandparents' house were not typical. Most of Sarah's
friends' grandmothers were much younger than Louella.

They were grandmothers who took their granddaughters to the mall or the movies.

Now, grown up, it pierces Sarah sharply to imagine Louella witnessing her self-centered, childish unrest at this realization, this *deprivation*, even though Louella might have understood it, maybe even anticipated it. Sarah recognized too late that what she had as a child was so much more, in that it was much less. She and Louella were never rushing here, there, and everywhere, buying anything, late for anything. At her grandparents' house, Sarah had a rare place to disassemble her usual self and just be.

Even with Louella gone, Sarah can find this shared peace again in the parts she's been able to keep, all the details reassembling in her memory. The steam in the tight kitchen, dinner cooking itself along. The brocade chair in the living room corner that spun all the way around to face the wall and back again. The slight tug of Louella's crooked fingers braiding her hair. The low creaking of the porch glider as Louella's foot pushed them back and forth in a lazy afternoon sway. The chill of early morning as they stepped together off the back stoop to toss bread to the birds.

Thirty-five

By the time Margaret moved Louella to the nursing home, Sarah was already in college. Then she had moved into her own apartment and found a job. Then she moved again, met Gavin, and then she was planning their wedding. She came home to her parents' house often, though, and when she was there, she always went with Margaret to visit Louella. Sarah visited her grandmother there only once by herself. She couldn't stand Bridgeway.

Sarah and Margaret had planned to go together that day, and then Margaret was caught up at a dentist appointment. Sarah had felt compelled to go, even though she was pretty sure Louella wouldn't recognize her. Sarah knew visiting her grandmother would quell some of the constant guilt Margaret endured, that black cloud of no good solution.

Sarah signed in at the front desk and walked down the hall, skirting all the wheelchairs and walkers. All those sad, trapped souls. She wanted to leave herself a wide buffer. She was revolted by the smells and the sounds, even as she berated herself for her repulsion. Sarah felt a deep ache seeing her grandmother here, knowing that this was her grandmother's home after all. After all the years Louella spent loving and caring for her own home just so, this was where she had ended up.

As Sarah was about to turn the corner leading to her grandmother's room, she saw Louella parked in her wheelchair in the common room straight ahead. This was odd. Louella almost never left her room. She lived so much inside her own head that her actual physical surroundings didn't seem to matter very much. Sarah felt her heart leap into her throat, and she tasted tears. Louella sat, hands folded motionless in her lap, her chin tilted up toward the television. Her attention was steady but her eyes were unfocused. As much as Sarah wished it, she knew Louella being in that room surrounded by other residents meant nothing. Nothing had changed.

And why should it have? Who would want to be engaged and aware in this kind of present, surrounded by drooling, muttering, shuffling companions, Sarah had thought. Who would want to know themselves part of this depressing landscape? Sarah reminded herself that each of these souls was also someone's parent or aunt or uncle, sister or brother, or grandparent to someone like her. Then again maybe they were no one to anyone anymore. For a moment she had felt an immense, swooping sadness for those lonely ones who didn't even have the company of a granddaughter they wouldn't recognize. Maybe it was much better that Louella lived mostly inside her own head, carried along by whatever connected her back to the young and able self she had been as a daughter, a sister, a wife, a mother.

Sarah walked ahead into the common room cautiously. She didn't want to make a ripple. No one in that room knew who she was, because no one really knew who Louella was. She was a non-entity in this sea of decay. When Sarah visited Bridgeway with her mother, Margaret always brought her minister self. She greeted the residents solicitously, usually by name, with a hand on a shoulder or a warm smile. Sarah couldn't do that, couldn't be that person. She would not spend any of the energy she'd mustered for this visit on anyone else. She was there for Louella, and only for Louella. Sarah would know it even if her grandmother did not.

Sarah knelt by the side of Louella's wheelchair and looked up into her grandmother's face. Louella turned to Sarah then, fully alert. She grasped Sarah's hand in both of hers. Her palms and fingers were warm and soft, just the way Sarah remembered them from childhood. Her touch didn't match the chilled, papery fragility of the rest of her.

"You came," Louella stated simply. She smiled a radiant smile, her real smile.

Sarah could not find words to answer her grandmother. Her tears dripped, silent and unchecked, down her face. *She couldn't have known I was coming,* Sarah thought, but she knew, without a doubt, that Louella had been sitting there waiting for her.

Just as swiftly as that smile had surfaced, it let go and was gone, dissolved back into the deep. Louella still rested her hands around Sarah's hand, but the firm, warm grasp was gone, and so was she.

"You're lovely. You are so sweet," she said. She looked vaguely at Sarah and patted her cheek.

Louella died two weeks later. When a wandering mind and a collection of delicate, sharp bones inside too much skin are all that's left of a body, death is not shocking. When everyone else is already gone, death is not tragic. Even so, death is always a loss for those left on the other side of it.

Louella was taken to the hospital for fluids and sedation after becoming inconsolable and incoherent. Margaret didn't get there in time to say goodbye. The nurses told Margaret afterward that Louella kept repeating how sorry she was. Over and over again, she was so, so sorry. Then she went silent and stopped breathing. Sarah knew Louella had been gone long before that. Her soul had already been roaming freely somewhere else for quite a while, just waiting for her body to follow.

Margaret asked Sarah to sing at Louella's funeral, but it was more a directive than a request. Picking their way down the frost-buckled sidewalk between the church and the funeral home the day after Louella's death, Margaret asked the question without looking at Sarah. It will just be something easy, something you know already, she had said.

Though the song Margaret chose was called *A Gift To Be Simple*, for Sarah it was not simple at all. She knew the song well, but as she began, as she saw glimmers of tears and watched tissues being pulled smoothly from purses, her eyes pricked and her throat constricted. Just as she'd known they would. There was no stopping it, no breathing through it, and she could barely continue over the lump in her throat.

Why had her mother asked her to do this, knowing that Sarah would not be able to say no, but also knowing Sarah? To Margaret, every issue in life was one to be conquered, to be overcome, bested. Nothing was to be simply accepted, everything was to be approached as a challenge. But she also knew that Sarah did not come at life this way at all. Didn't she?

Sarah had closed her eyes for the rest of the song. Methodically, she'd pictured the page of music, the notes of the score, the words following along underneath. She followed along with them until she reached the end. Was her mother moved, too? Crying, too? She would never know. She could not look at Margaret for the rest of the service.

Thirty-six

On Sunday afternoon, Sarah sits on the couch in her front room, staring intently out the large picture window, watching for Margaret. The house is shut tight against the hot world outside, Sarah sealed in while everything else is sealed out. The only sound is the hushed whoosh of the air conditioning, distinct and luxurious. She's twitchy sitting there, despite the cool air inside and the restful scene outside, the greening spring lawn and magnificent maple standing sentry in the center of their wide front yard.

Sarah always feels anxious waiting for her mother to get there, even on days more ordinary than today. Whenever her parents visit, Sarah feels sort of like the homesick girl she was away at college for the first time. Whenever her parents came out to see her at school, and then left for home again without her, Sarah would be washed over with waves of emptiness. They were returning to a life that wasn't hers to claim anymore, and she didn't feel quite yet like her life at school was completely hers either.

Now when her parents visit her, she's swept again with that familiar empty feeling, but now it's for the loss of the child she was, the loss of her complete need to belong to her first family as only a child does. Sarah knows she's right where she belongs, making her home, loving her husband, waiting for her baby. But now there's this new kind of bittersweet when the old kind fails to bloom.

Sarah gets up as soon as she sees Margaret's car come around the corner and pull into her street. She stands, fixed and watchful, as her mother stops the car in the driveway and gets out. Then she recovers herself and goes into the kitchen. She knows Margaret will let herself in.

Margaret knocks on the front door, then opens it and steps inside. She calls out hello just as Sarah puts a pitcher of cold lemonade on the dining room table. Droplets of lemony sweat slide uncaring onto the table's bare surface.

Since her visit with Lida, Sarah has been keeping company with something distinctly other. Her mother feels it, too, Sarah thinks now, sensing an unfamiliar hesitation it in the way Margaret approaches her, arms outstretched, offering a large shopping bag.

"Do you want some lemonade?" Sarah asks.

"No," Margaret answer quickly. "Let's take out the blanket."

Sarah pulls out a chair, and Margaret sets the bag down in it. Together they lift out the package, so ordinary looking in its brown paper wrapping. Sarah lays it flat on the table. She remembers the blanket, knows from memory the texture of the white crochet work, both soft and solid, the colorful roses springing with relief from their background. She'd wrapped many dreams up in this blanket once upon a time.

The package is held closed with a length of simple brown ribbon of some kind. Sarah unties it, and the paper falls open. Folded within a layer of white tissue paper is the blanket. On top of it sits a bundle of notepaper, tied with the same brown trimming.

"What is this?" Sarah asks her mother as she sees her name on the outside. *Sarah* is written in Louella's loopy script, not Margaret's controlled, efficient writing.

Margaret responds with a small smile.

"I don't really know. I didn't open it, since it has your name on it."

Sarah feels the air stir. She wonders if Margaret feels it, too. Or was it just her imagination? Moments ago, she would have been reluctant to trade the cool sanctuary of her house for anywhere else, but suddenly she's chilled.

"Let's go out to the porch," Sarah says. Holding the blanket to her body, paper and letter and all, she walks to the porch door without waiting for her mother to respond. Margaret follows. Sarah sits heavily down in the wicker chair. The blanket, weighty on her lap, feels just right despite the close, hot air of the porch. Margaret pulls over a squeaky metal patio chair and sits down as Sarah unfolds the thick sheaf of lined paper from its bundle.

"Do you want me to read it out loud?" she asks.

"Yes," Margaret says almost before the question is complete.

Sarah unfolds the papers

Her eyes adjust to the familiar, scrawling handwriting. This writing had made lined paper, the very kind of paper she holds now, into grocery lists and quick notes to her grandfather. It had made birthday cards into mementoes. It had signed hundreds of Christmas cards. But she has never seen so much of it all at once. The swoops and scrawls resolve into words, words Sarah shares with her mother in the heat of that still afternoon.

Thirty-seven

Dear Sarah,

Loss is inevitable. I have come to know this inescapable truth all too well. The grief that follows is bearable. But how to bear it? That question is answered differently by each one of us. How will you furrow despite your sorrows? Will you succeed at planting life and grief together side by side? Because that is what can nearly tear you in two, the plowing of this pathway through your soul. Will the sky above you expand to let light in once again, or will it press itself in heavy all around you, letting nothing new grow? Grief and joy, the weights of time, propel our lives forward and back and forward again. The moments of my life have contracted and expanded, and now they are all but used up. All the days, all the layers, stack and compress like so much sediment, until each day becomes the merest sliver. Most of them are just regular, necessary rock. But some are shiny and precious, and they will remain, while the rest just silt away.

I think I've learned that for most of us, real joy can only exist with an underpinning of sorrow. For me, those who came after my losses – your grandfather, your mother, and then you – have brought me that real joy, have brought more true happiness than I ever could have thought possible for myself once upon a time. But first there was loss. Mine was a loss I never truly surfaced from until you became my granddaughter. I was not the mother I really wanted to be to Margaret. I was too afraid to let go, and at the same time too afraid to hold her as close as I really wanted to. There was something in the way, an old, old stone lodged deep in my heart. I was guilty and afraid. I couldn't forgive myself, and my fear shaped everything I was. It especially shaped who I was to your mother.

When I was young, just nineteen years old, I was married to a man named Holland Richards. Your mother knows this much. I loved him truly in the way of all young love. He was funny and captivating, both handsome and sweet. Life was always sunny for Holland, and this light surrounded my life, too. But then Holland died. Pneumonia. We were only married for two short months. Your mother knows this part, also. But what she doesn't know is that I was pregnant when Holland died. The following summer, I had a baby boy. I named him Holland after his father. I was in a pit of grief, living in my childhood home again, all at once a widow and a mother, and too young and sad for it all. I gave the baby to my sister Angelica to raise. My mother and Angelica both convinced me this would be the best thing for the baby, and for me, too. Giving the baby over to Angelica may seem surprising to you, but people did this then, gave up children to be raised by relatives, or sometimes even strangers, for many reasons, if it seemed the best course for that child. But this did not turn out to be the best course for my child.

The baby lived with Angelica and her husband, Arthur, for a short time, just a few months. And then he, too, died, before I ever saw him again. I was too undone to even travel to his funeral. I know now that his death was not my fault, was not anyone's fault really. Babies got sick and died much more regularly then than they do now. Even so, I was overwhelmed with guilt. If any pieces of my heart were beginning to mend themselves, they were fragile fixes, and this loss broke them right apart again. I was appalled by how willingly I had let my baby go. I was heartsick, heartbroken. I can use those words, but they only begin to scratch at the surface of my despair. There really are no right words. I imagined that if the baby had stayed with me, he wouldn't have died. I felt as if his death were a direct result of my giving him up, as if I had given up on him. After that, I kept the door to that room in my heart firmly barred, trapping that hard, heavy weight of guilt and regret that was mine and mine alone.

I will never know what kind of mother I would have been to Margaret if these experiences had been different, or had not been at all, or if I had mustered the courage to share this story better, sooner. If Holland had stayed with me, had been healthy and grown up, there might never have been a Margaret who was my daughter. We can only wonder at the many paths laid out before us. We can only wonder if, in the end, they might all just connect and lead to the same destination.

But I thought it best to keep my story inside, to press it all down deep, and to press on. I've realized by watching you with your mother and loving you so much myself that it was not the best choice. I never pushed your mother to do anything she wasn't inclined toward. She was very definite anyway about what she did and did not want to do. I think I worried that if I pushed her to do something she didn't want to do, I might also push her completely away from me. Of course, every child leaves anyway, as it should be. It happens oh so much swifter than you think it will. Then it doesn't matter how tightly you've held on or how easily you've let go. And all the worrying about the what ifs and the threatening possibilities does nothing but deplete you, making you less prepared for the real dangers and losses when they do come.

Once she was grown up, I could have told your mother the story of the baby, of the brother she didn't know she'd had, but at every turn, every opportunity, I imagined how my revelation might make her feel. Laying my guilt at her feet never seemed right or fair. It should not be a child's place, even an adult child, to offer absolution. I've come to see that my telling Margaret could have revealed a better path for us, marked and difficult, but loving and true, especially once Margaret was a mother, once she had you.

The space between your mother and me is too wide even now, and that's why I'm writing this letter for you and not your mother. This letter is meant for you when you're grown up, when you are a mother yourself. By then Margaret will be on the other side of motherhood. I think, I hope, maybe she will better understand me, and have sympathy and forgiveness for my faults. You are only four as I'm writing this letter, and even at this early point I can see that Margaret is a better mother than I ever was to her. But even in all my failing moments, in all my wrong choices, I have always loved her in all the spaces of my heart, as she does you, and as you will your waiting child.

Grandma

Thirty-eight

The pages of Louella's letter finally do run empty, the words pooling in Sarah's heart. Margaret and Sarah sit in silence for a long time, alone together. They are tearstained, battered, suspended in simultaneous bewilderment and recognition by this story that had waited so long, so patiently, so far beneath the surface.

In the measured time between discovering Louella's letter and the day Sarah's baby is ready to be born, Sarah spends many hours like this, just sitting, lost in her own wondering and wandering, in curious thought and questioning. She is about to become someone's mother. With each passing day, she is more and more confident that she's up to the job, even as she realizes with growing certainty that it's one to be done, one she will do, almost entirely by feel.

Science and modern medicine fortify us with knowledge and understanding. They expand our abilities to bend the world we live in around our needs and wants. Yet the facts we prove with science and study are still not equal to all we cannot see, but somehow know is there.

At her twenty-week ultrasound the doctor had told Sarah and Gavin that they were going to have a girl, and Sarah didn't have any reason to question that concrete, medical fact. Yet on the August night when her baby finally arrives, neither does she question the tiny boy placed gently in her arms.

Holland is not a common name, not a name you run across very often. But Sarah thinks this boy of hers will grow into his name very well. He belongs to Sarah, he belongs in the here and now, but he also carries within him pieces of everything that came before him and made it so.

Postscript

Louella Reams was my grandmother. Putting aside the necessary copyright page disclaimer, much of this story is true, gathered from what I remember her telling me and what my mother has added over the years. I've taken some liberties with the details, shaping the facts and figures around my childhood memories to fit the story in my heart.

In the microcosm of my grandmother's long life there existed an entire world to which I now have only imaginary access. My parents tell me that when I was a child, I measured time into three categories: when dinosaurs were alive, when Grandma was a little girl, and present day. I was often incredulous that my grandmother had almost been born in the previous century, and I plugged away at her with a child's questions about living on a farm, and about whether she was sure she didn't have some *Little House on the Prairie* type relics like high button shoes or china dolls tucked away in the attic somewhere.

Now, as an adult, there are so many deeper, more personal, more poignant items of inquiry on my list. Of course, I'm too late.

Louella's life was ordinary in so many ways, but it was also so full of the wonderful and tragic, full of big, sweeping experiences. In this way, I think her life is an example of all our lives, really. We're all plain and ordinary. We all start out and end the same way, yet we all live a wealth of dramatic experiences within the scope of our everyday, individual lives.

The Reams family was large even by early twentieth century farm standards. Born in 1903, Louella was really the eighth of *seventeen* children. There were the boys: Roy, Howard, John, Sylvester, Austin, Marshall, Kenneth, and Carrol. And there were the girls: Gracie, Edith, Jane, Susie, Verna, Lenore, Dorothy, Louella, and Caroline. My grandmother could tick off all their names like she was reciting the alphabet. I've shrunk the family size in this story to be able to handle the necessary characters inside a small story deftly, focusing on those most vital to me.

My grandmother really did grow up on a farm in Osceola Mills, Pennsylvania. When I was a kid, The Middle Of Nowhere was how I defined that dreary, claustrophobic place. Our visits were always during summer, and it was always "hot as Hades," and those relatives had never even heard of air conditioning, central or window. I was so relieved when it was time to pile back into the car and drive home to New Jersey. Funny how life works out. Now I live, quite happily most days, with my own family in sort of *the middle of nowhere* Pennsylvania.

Louella was widowed just two months after her first marriage, while pregnant with her first child, whom one of her sisters did offer to adopt. But, stalwart and grounded, my grandmother raised the baby herself. That is an incredible, deeply affecting experience I really wish I had talked to her more about. I've realized while writing this book, now that I'm grown up and a mother myself, that the most moving, dramatic, difficult, and transformative parts of Louella's life were not the grandiose events she witnessed during her lifetime – both World Wars, the Great Depression, new-fangled inventions like cars and televisions. It's the individual, personal experiences that mold our internal landscapes. For most of us, the historic events unfolding around us are just the backdrop.

Louella married my grandfather, Sam Pusey, when she was forty. They moved to New Jersey while Sam was part of the US Army Signal Corps during World War II. This was, apparently, much to the consternation of Sam's very difficult mother, Willetta Copenhaver Pusey. My mother was born when my grandmother was forty-two. Louella's son, Hobert Richards, my mother's half-brother who was very much alive and not given away, was nineteen, almost grown up, when my mother was born. My grandparents and mother moved, ultimately, into the house my grandfather built for them on Crest Avenue in Haddon Heights. He was a hard-working, determined, and often solitary man, and completed almost all the work on the house himself – including, I'm sure, the plumbing!

I visited that house, my mother's childhood home, several years ago on a warm Sunday afternoon in May with my parents, my brother and his baby daughter, and my two older children. My mother had wanted to make this pilgrimage for a long time. She'd contacted the family living there, the same family she'd sold the house to after my grandmother died, and they were more than happy to welcome us there for a visit. There were small pieces of me that were curious about what the house would look like, and what it would feel like to walk though it again, about what memories might resurface.

But a much larger piece of my heart didn't want to be there at all. During my childhood, that house was the place of ultimate safety, comfort, and withdrawal from the world. I couldn't step through its present-day front door without the tears coming fast and hard, and I had to step back outside and sit down on the stoop. I missed my grandmother that day more sharply than I had in a long time. And I missed the child I had been in that place.

The house had changed in the real world, but I decided that day not to let it change in my memory. I decided to recreate it and Louella's world here, in this book.

I've also truly recounted my visit with a psychic friend who encouraged me to come for a reading when I was pregnant with my third child. I've changed her name and description in this story, but her attributes are equally lovely inside and out, to those of my invented character, Lida. My session with her was the first time I'd ever had a for-real reading. What my friend told me during that reading about my grandmother and the rose covered blanket, as well as my mother's response when I called her afterwards, is portrayed in these pages as it really happened. That unbidden revelation provided my need to write about Louella's life with the springboard to make it a good story.

I've surely heard my grandmother's voice inside my head as I've woven this tale. As I sat in my front room one rain-soaked October morning writing away, a little bird visited around my front door. She was dark-bodied and rose-breasted, moving too fast for me to see clearly, hopping and chirping, and then flying away. I decided to believe she was just there to say hello, to check in.

Acknowledgements

In the last two years, I've dedicated so much time to this book – writing and rewriting, outlining and editing, reorganizing and workshopping, submitting and ... and, and, and. Conjuring a story, developing it, and then making a book out if it necessitates so many *ands*. Some days it feels like the *ands* will be endless, and you wonder if you'll ever hold the actual product in your hand and say *DONE!*

Thank you to my family for giving me space and support and smiles. Thank you for asking, "How's the book going?" just often enough. I'm proud of this book, but it's just a book. You – Jim, Owen, Claire, and Katie – are my story.

Thank you to my good friends, diligent readers, and extended family, who all encouraged my process from start to finish.

Thank you to my mother, Kathryn Henry, for digging up the family letters and photos that helped shape the characters of Louella and Sam.

And thank you to David Caslow for enthusiastically sharing photos and articles from the Osceola Mills Historical Museum. Your copy is on its way.

About the author

Elizabeth Dougherty lives and writes in Chester County, Pennsylvania. Her essays and stories chronicle the comical, stressful, mundane, tearful, and astounding elements of every day, and how they all tie together to define our lives.

To read more, please visit Plan Q at
www.elizabethdoughertyfreelancewriting.wordpress.com

A Robin's Pageant is her first novel.

Made in the USA
Middletown, DE
02 October 2018